Dead Hot Mama

"Enough to make anyone long for the scent of pines. An addictive series . . . A complicated mystery with plenty of red herrings (and a few muskies) . . . that will have readers guessing up until the last minute. Another strong entry into a very atmospheric and entertaining series that will have even the most sun-worshipping readers consider digging a hole in the ice, dropping a line in and hoping for a bite."
—*The Mystery Reader*

Dead Frenzy

"Houston has a way with words . . . Her humor is well rationed . . . The good doctor is a pleasant, witty voice. The description of a fishing experience is well done, depicting the Northwoods to a 'T.' The mystery is plotted well, and there is enough action to keep the reader engaged to the end. The Loon Lake series holds great promise for a pleasurable reading retreat."
—*Books 'n' Bytes*

Dead Water

"*Dead Water* is her best yet . . . [Victoria Houston] puts me right there in the Wisconsin heat and cold, lets me know what the fish are biting on, lets me spy on the interesting characters of Loon Lake, and most of all, spins an intelligent and captivating tale. I look forward to more and more."
—T. Jefferson Parker, author of *Silent Joe*

"Victoria Houston's love for her Wisconsin setting—and her wonderful characters—is evident on every page of her fine series . . . A great getaway, even if it does keep me up at night."
—Laura Lippman, author of *The Sugar House*

continued . . .

Dead Creek

"[A] well-drawn regional police procedural . . . All the subplots smoothly return to the main theme and there are plenty of suspects to keep the audience guessing . . . With this fine novel, Victoria Houston will hook readers and make them seek her previous stories."

—*Painted Rock Reviews*

"What a great story! A book that fishermen of all ages (and species) are sure to enjoy." —Tony Rizzo,
Northwoods fishing guide
and author of *Secrets of a Muskie Guide*

"Murder mystery muskies! The *X-Files* comes to Packer Land." —John Krga,
dedicated Northwoods "catch-and-release" muskie fisherman

Dead Angler

"Who would have thought that fly-fishing could be such fun? Victoria Houston makes you want to dash for rod and reel. [She] cleverly blends the love of the outdoors with the thrill of catching a serial killer." —*The Orlando Sentinel*

Dead Jitterbug

VICTORIA HOUSTON

BERKLEY PRIME CRIME, NEW YORK

THE BERKLEY PUBLISHING GROUP
Published by the Penguin Group
Penguin Group (USA) Inc.
375 Hudson Street, New York, New York 10014, USA
Penguin Group (Canada), 10 Alcorn Avenue, Toronto, Ontario M4V 3B2, Canada
(a division of Pearson Penguin Canada Inc.)
Penguin Books Ltd., 80 Strand, London WC2R 0RL, England
Penguin Group Ireland, 25 St. Stephen's Green, Dublin 2, Ireland (a division of Penguin Books Ltd.)
Penguin Group (Australia), 250 Camberwell Road, Camberwell, Victoria 3124, Australia
(a division of Pearson Australia Group Pty. Ltd.)
Penguin Books India Pvt. Ltd., 11 Community Centre, Panchsheel Park, New Delhi—110 017, India
Penguin Group (NZ), Cnr. Airborne and Rosedale Roads, Albany, Auckland 1310, New Zealand
(a division of Pearson New Zealand Ltd.)
Penguin Books (South Africa) (Pty.) Ltd., 24 Sturdee Avenue, Rosebank, Johannesburg 2196,
South Africa

Penguin Books Ltd., Registered Offices: 80 Strand, London WC2R 0RL, England

DEAD JITTERBUG

A Berkley Prime Crime Book / published by arrangement with the author

PRINTING HISTORY
Berkley Prime Crime edition / April 2005

Copyright © 2005 by Victoria Houston.
Cover design by Steve Ferlauto.
Cover illustration by Dan Craig.

ISBN: 0-425-20201-1

BERKLEY PRIME CRIME®
Berkley Prime Crime Books are published by The Berkley Publishing Group,
a division of Penguin Group (USA) Inc.,
375 Hudson Street, New York, New York 10014.
BERKLEY PRIME CRIME is a registered trademark of Penguin Group (USA) Inc.
The Berkley Prime Crime design is a trademark belonging to Penguin Group (USA) Inc.

PRINTED IN THE UNITED STATES OF AMERICA

10 9 8 7 6 5 4 3 2 1

For John

one

How cheerfully he seems to grin,
How neatly spreads his claws,
And welcomes little fishes in
With gently smiling jaws!

—Lewis Carroll

The two kids knew better than to go where they went. It's one thing to fish off your own dock, quite another to park yourself at the end of someone else's. And while it can be argued that in Wisconsin no one owns the lakes and the rivers, it's also understood that the water in front of your land is private. At least the first hundred feet.

But the girl and her little brother had lately elected to ignore that unwritten rule. Partly because they were bored, partly because they couldn't resist the challenge of the feisty smallmouth bass hunkered down under the pontoon boat moored to the end of the McDonalds' long dock.

It was Jennifer who kept urging them to go one more time, well aware you can't be arrested for wading. Not even wading with a spinning rod unless you're sixteen and trying to fish without a license.

But the smallies weren't the only lure for Jennifer.

She knew that Mrs. McDonald was a famous lady and rich. Very rich. It was the rich that fascinated Jennifer. She loved to wade slowly through the hip-deep water about thirty feet out from the McDonalds' beach, close enough to take in every detail of the big sprawling house.

Built by Mrs. McDonald's grandfather in the early 1900's, the mansion was one of the few on the Loon Lake chain and visible only from the water. And even water access was not easy as the old man had bought himself property on a 300-acre lake that connected to the chain through a channel so shallow few fishermen were willing to risk ruining their propellers.

With its white frame and forest-green shutters, whose Christmas tree cutouts emphasized its whiteness, the stately home looked like something out of a storybook with its gabled windows and romantic balconies. A white banister porch ran along the entire front of the house, and pots of pink petunias with English ivy cascaded over the handrails, inviting visitors from the lake. An ancient stone stairway snaking up from the dock was bordered on both sides by a lawn, deep green and perfectly trimmed.

At dusk, thanks to the glow of interior lights, the girl was often able to see the outlines of an elegant dining room just inside the French doors. More than once she had glimpsed Mrs. McDonald at the big table, dining alone.

Jennifer liked to pretend it was her house. That she could skip through the water, boost herself up onto the dock, dance up those stone stairs, and be welcomed into what she knew must be the most magnificent home in Loon Lake. Dusk was her favorite time to drop a

worm and a bobber and linger out front. She brought
her brother along just in case someone got upset. Who
could be mad at a little boy and his sister trying to
catch a couple crappies or fierce-fighting bass?

Tonight, the third night in a row that they had waded
down this way, Jennifer was surprised to see Mrs.
McDonald sitting at her dining room table in exactly
the same spot she had been the night before. And the
night before that. Even the low glow of the chandelier
appeared identical to what she had seen each previous
evening.

"Yow!" Timmy yanked his rod up and back, reeling
fast. "Jenny, it's big, it's really big."

"Keep your line tight," said Jennifer, absently. The
overcast sky made the evening darker than usual for
early June, emphasizing the dimly lit interior of the big
house. The longer she stared, the more Jennifer was
convinced that woman had not moved since they saw
her last. And she certainly wasn't moving now.

While Timmy struggled with his catch, Jennifer
edged closer to shore. She might be just nine years old
but she was used to taking charge. Their mother
worked evenings waiting tables at the Loon Lake Pub,
and their dad lived in the neighboring town with his
new family, so Jennifer was responsible for Timmy and
the dog every day from six to midnight. She liked to
think of herself as capable and fearless, though right
now she was worried. And not a little scared.

Mrs. McDonald knew her. The lady, who had very
pretty white hair and was a lot older than Jennifer's
mom, always waved if she saw Jennifer as she walked
across the road to fetch her mail from the huge mailbox

that dwarfed all the others on the lake road. Summertime, she got her mail every day at the same time. But she hadn't done so today, and Jennifer hadn't been home to see if she had the day before.

Jennifer gave herself two options: On the one hand she could wade home, peek in the McDonalds' mailbox, and if it was empty she would know the lady was all right. Of course, how could she be sure that there had been any mail that day? Or she could walk up onto the porch, knock on the French doors and say that Timmy had stuck himself with his fishhook and they needed a Band-Aid. The second option was the best: the quickest, the easiest, and, if she was lucky, she might even be invited inside.

Feeling a little less worried, Jennifer set her rod on the dock, hopped across the stones at the water's edge, and walked up onto the beach. She stopped and waved her arms at the figure in the window. No response.

"Jenny, where are you going?" asked Timmy, just as his fishing pole, bent low by the fighting fish, popped into the air. "Darn! Bit right through my line." He waded toward his sister. "Wait for me. Do you have another hook on you? Man, that must've been a muskie to bite right through my line like that. Took my hook, worm, sinker even. Still got my bobber, though."

The resolute tone in the seven-year-old's voice made it clear he would treat this loss as a win. He didn't lose some little bass, no sirree. He just survived a strike from the one of the biggest fish you can catch on the Loon Lake chain. Man, oh man. That would get his dad's attention for sure.

Jennifer waved her brother over to the dock. From the back pocket of her wet cutoffs, she pulled out a Sucrets tin. Inside writhed half a dozen angleworms, and taped to the bottom of the tin were two fishing lures. The tin was a gift from their mother's childhood pal, and sometime boyfriend, Ray Pradt.

Ray was a fishing guide and a stickler for not hauling along too much tackle. And he was the only grown-up who had not criticized her habit of wading along the shore to fish other people's holes. Nope, he had just winked and warned her to be sure to get out fast the minute she saw any lightning.

"Here, Timmy." She thrust the tin into her brother's hand. "Be right back. Gotta ask Mrs. McDonald a question. You tie on one of those lures and wait for me here."

"But I don't have a sinker," said Timmy, a long look on his face.

"So? You don't need a sinker with one of Ray's lures."

Before her brother could protest, Jennifer was running up the stone stairs and onto the porch, waving her arms as she neared the French doors. She was right, it was Mrs. McDonald—she could tell from the white hair. But the woman was sitting slightly slumped with her head turned away.

Jennifer rapped on the glass door. Mrs. McDonald didn't move. What appeared to be a full plate of food was set in front of where she sat at the far end of the long table that ran parallel to the doors. The low glow of the chandelier threw shadows into the room, making it difficult to get a good look at the seated figure.

Worry and fear crowded back into Jennifer's chest. What if Mrs. McDonald was sick or something and that's why she didn't turn around? The girl debated trying the handle on the door, which she knew was trespassing, or just going home and pretending she hadn't been here or seen anything. But the urge to help was overwhelming.

She reminded herself that Mrs. McDonald had always smiled and waved. And Jennifer's mom had said that she was very famous and did wonderful things for people. What those wonderful things were, Jennifer didn't know—but if you did good things for others maybe you wouldn't be too mad if someone tried to help you. . . .

She pushed down on the handle. It was locked. Jennifer rapped harder on the glass door and called out, "Mrs. McDonald?" Still, the lady didn't move. Jennifer knew she couldn't stop now. She called louder and waited. Still no answer. Floor to ceiling windows extended along the wall beyond the French doors, so she moved along the porch until she was directly across from the woman.

A break in the cloud cover sent rays from the setting sun slanting across the table and Jennifer could see that Mrs. McDonald hadn't been looking away at all. The side of her head was gone. No, it wasn't. Something was there: something black and twisted and moving.

Jennifer froze, then flew from the porch and across the lawn.

"Timmy! Timmy!" Her screams turned into sobs. "Run!" At the sound of his sister's terror, Timmy burst into tears. The two of them could never remember how they got home, but they made it. Not until the next morning did Jennifer remember that she left her Sucrets tin on the McDonalds' dock.

two

Fish or cut bait.

—Anonymous

The security service for the McDonald estate rang the Loon Lake Police Department within five minutes of someone exerting pressure on the handle to the French doors.

It was June fourth, seven forty-five in the evening, and Loon Lake Chief of Police Lewellyn Ferris was going over her schedule for the next six weeks with her campaign manager. Erin was not happy. The election was slated for August sixth, and her candidate was already two weeks behind on public outreach.

"Lewellyn," said Erin, dropping the more formal "Chief," which she should have used. Or even the less formal "Lew," which she used when her father included Lewellyn Ferris in family gatherings. "Lewellyn, if you want to be elected sheriff of Lake County, you have got to go door to door and shake every hand. I'm dead serious."

Erin emphasized her words with a pointed index finger. "You're paying me to run this campaign—so I'm doing my level best to give you what you pay for. But if you don't follow my directions, you are wasting your money and my time. Didn't I take a break from summer school to do this?"

Lew teased Erin with a questioning look. She could get away with the first statement but not the latter. They both knew she needed the break from law school. With three children, a husband who was a practicing attorney, and a Victorian house in constant need of repair, Erin welcomed having her summer back. Plus she loved politics.

"I hear you," said Lew, raising her right hand in surrender. "I'll do it, I promise."

"Okay, then here's the deal. Set a daily quota of hands you shake *before* you go fishing with Dad," said Erin, leaning forward in her chair. "That is the only way you're going to cover this county in time."

Lew winced. "But not tonight, kiddo. Not when there's a weather change like this one coming in. The conditions will be *perfect* for muskie. Wind from the right direction for trying my fly rod—and you know that doesn't happen too often."

"Tonight's okay. Too late to knock on doors anyway. But every day from here on in, the minute you're off duty—between five and seven P.M., plus your lunch hour. If you'll do that, we'll—"

The intercom buzzed as Marlene, the switchboard operator, interrupted with news of a possible break-in on the McDonald property. "Their security has called the house twice and no answer," she said. "They insist we check on it."

"How many false alarms have we had on that one?" asked Lew, too familiar with flower-addicted deer and inquisitive bears to get excited.

"None. Ever. I checked," said Marlene.

Her answer caused Lew to sit up straight. "Oh, then I better check it out. Give Roger a call and let him know he's got to cover for me the next hour or so, will you? He's not due in until nine."

"The McDonald place?" asked Erin, eyes wide as Lew set down the phone. "The big house on Secret Lake? That's not far from Dad's by water—but half an hour or more if you have to take the road in."

Lew picked up the phone and asked for an outside line. She waited. "No answer. Where do you think your dad is? I'm supposed to meet him," she glanced at her watch, "in less than an hour for whatever night fishing we can squeeze in before the storm hits."

"He's probably still over at Ray's," said Erin. "I called this morning just as he was going out the door. Ray conned him into helping out with that 'Fishing For Girls' class of his—"

Before Erin could finish, Lew was ringing the phone in Ray's trailer home.

"You know who Mrs. McDonald is, don't you?" asked Erin while Lew let the phone ring. Ray was notorious for owning an answering machine of dubious reliability and no cell phone. Assuming he might be out on the dock, if not still on the lake with his students, it could take a few rings to get an answer.

"No luck. I better drive out there," said Lew, reaching for the jacket to her uniform, which hung on a coat rack near the door to her office. "You're right about the roads—I can save time if I take your father's boat over." Erin ran behind Lew as she hurried down the hall and out the front door to the parking lot.

"Who did you say these McDonalds are?" asked

Lew, opening the door to her police cruiser. "They put the fear of God into the security people. Poor guy told Marlene he'll lose his job if I don't show up ASAP."

"The wife is Hope McDonald Kelly—she goes by her maiden name. You know, the famous advice-columnist. The one you read in the *Loon Lake Daily News*. Eighty million readers worldwide every day."

Lew looked at her in astonishment. "You're kidding."

"Nope. Not too many people know that either. I guess she hides out up here all summer—has for years. Ask Dad, he knows the family. They were summer patients."

three

Rains pour down without water,
and the rivers are streams of light.
One love it is
that pervades the world;
few there are who know it fully.

—Kabir

The first hint that his Tuesday might not go according to plan was the call from Ray at five forty-five that morning: "Hey, Doc, how's it goin'?"

Osborne cleared his throat. "Other than the fact you just woke me up?"

"Sorry about that. Had to catch you before you headed into town. How . . . would you like . . . to earn . . . a few buckaroos today, Doc?" Ray vested each word with the importance of a winning lottery ticket.

"Okay—what's wrong?" asked Osborne, not a little cranky and clutching the cordless to his ear as he stumbled toward the porch to let the dog out. The fishing guide, so chronically short of cash that he dug graves to make ends meet, had something up that crisply ironed khaki sleeve of his. No one in their right mind pays a retired dentist to dip minnows and hook leeches.

Six years living next door to the guy, Osborne knew all the red flags: an offer of cold cash as opposed to a string of fresh bluegills was not good news.

Gazing west through the porch windows while he listened, Osborne checked the conditions on the water. Sixty-three years into life, and fishing made him a better weather predictor than any of the jokers on TV.

Now that he had Osborne's attention, Ray spoke fast. "Doc, these gals are paying a hundred fifty each plus very nice tips, I'm sure. I have no problem giving you seventy-five and, brother, do I need the help. Five lovely ladies on one pontoon learning to cast? No way I can handle that all by myself. Not without someone getting hooked in the ear."

"Hold on there, big fella," said Osborne with a chuckle. "Am I not talking to a man who's been known to juggle half a dozen close female friendships simultaneously?"

"Not the same thing, Doc. These are five adult women about to be let loose with multihooked muskie lures *after* mainlining way too much coffee. This . . . could be . . . a *safety* sit-u-a-tion and . . . it worries me."

Osborne said nothing. This was classic Ray: exaggerating words and pauses until his listener would plead for a punch line. Only this time Osborne owned the punch line. He relished the moment.

"Please, Doc . . . Seventy-five . . . buckaroos."

It had all started when a reporter for the *Loon Lake Daily News*, researching a Sunday feature on local fishing guides, decided to pick up on a comment Ray made on how single women could meet more guys if only they knew how to fish.

"Think about it," he quoted Ray as saying, "hundreds, maybe thousands, of single guys rich enough to own their own boats up here in the northwoods every weekend all summer long. Now *that*, ladies, is opportunity."

By the end of the interview, egged on by the reporter, he had decided to offer a two-day seminar: "On catching fish, not guys. I'll call it . . . umm . . . 'Fishing For Girls.' "

This mushroomed into a sidebar to the main story that detailed not only what Ray would teach but included his home phone number along with a color photo of the thirty-four-year-old single white male wearing a stuffed trout on his head and holding a forty-eight-inch muskie.

Osborne suspected it wasn't the muskie that prompted the deluge of phone calls. And it wasn't the fish on his head. It was Ray. Tall, lean, tan Ray Pradt with his dark-brown curls just visible under the brim bearing the stuffed trout. It was the easy grin, the friendly eyes, and the flash of white teeth framed by the beard, curly and flecked rust and gray.

Ben Kaupinnen, one of the McDonald's coffee crowd that Osborne met with most mornings around six thirty, summed it up when he said, "You give that razzbonya (meaning Ray Pradt) just two dimensions (meaning a flat photo), and he can charm the living daylights out of a gal. Not to mention her pocketbook."

The Sunday that the newspaper story ran on the front page of the "Outdoors" section, Ray's phone never stopped ringing. Two calls were from teenagers who got a kick out of pretending they thought Ray's clinic was all about trolling for babes—the rest were from interested babes.

The story had legs all the way into the next week as three irritated readers peppered the *Loon Lake Daily News*' "Monday Mailbag" with anonymous letters complaining that the name of the seminar was tasteless. That it implied Ray was offering tips on Internet dating or how to find websites with unsavory content: "Not suitable for a family newspaper!"

Once Osborne's daughter, Erin, assured him that "any publicity is great publicity," Ray relished every call and complaint even as he signed up a total of twenty-four women for seminars to be offered mid-week over the next six weeks. The fact that he had never done this before didn't faze him. Nor the local merchants: Ralph's Sporting Goods agreed to let his students sample their rods and tackle; the local marina said they would provide a boat.

"All right, all right, let me check my calendar for the day," said Osborne, taking his time as he picked up his mug of hot coffee and walked back through the living room to the porch. He bent to look through the window once more.

The lake was serene, streaked with muted shades of rose and lavender stolen from the clouds overhead. Early summer breezes teased the curtains. He watched Mike chase two chipmunks across the yard. Hard as he tried every morning, the black lab never won that race.

Osborne inhaled. If you counted the promise in the air, this could be a very good day to be on water. And the evening looked good as well. He had plans to wade the weed beds off his dock, fly rod in hand. His favorite fishing partner had promised to give him some pointers on fly-fishing for muskie. Nope, life didn't get much better than this. He could spare a little of his good humor.

"Okay—looks like I can put a few things off. But forget the cash. How 'bout one of these nights, you sauté up some walleye cheeks with a side of that wild rice casserole of yours for Lew and myself?"

"Deal. Can you be here by seven-thirty?"

"Sure. How many women did you say there are?"

"Five. I had four booked and squeezed another one in at the last minute. All beginners. Never touched a spinning rod before yesterday. And, hey, Doc, just for fun I got a pop quiz for you. You get it right, and I'll enhance your little dinner party with a thimbleberry pie."

"Forget it. I said I'd help you out and that's enough," said Osborne, wincing as he poured himself a second mug of black coffee. He hated Ray's guessing games. Everyone hated them. Like Mike with the chipmunks, you never won.

"You gotta listen, Doc, this is right up your alley. Just take a minute. Ready?"

"No, I am not. Forget the quiz. Let me drink my coffee, get showered, and see you in an hour. I like to start the day happy."

"C'mon. You're the father of two daughters. You'll ace this. Now here's the deal. Yesterday we spent the day studying fish and their habitat, basic equipment, yadda, yadda. The usual stuff, right?"

Osborne sipped from his mug, eyebrows raised, waiting.

"However . . . I decided we would begin with . . . a

little philosophy. Kinda Zen-like, y'know? Some thoughts on *why* we fish." Osborne rolled his eyes.

"So first thing yesterday I had each one write on a slip of paper *why* she signed up for the class. Tonight, after we've had fun all day, I'll cook up our catch, and when we've eaten, I'll read each little slip. The ladies will have to guess who wrote what . . . and. . . ."

"And?" asked Osborne, anxious to hurry the story along.

"And whether or not the writer still feels the same way about fishing. These two days could change their lives, doncha know."

"Ray, the ladies signed up for a fishing seminar— not rehab."

Ray ignored Osborne's remark. "Let me tell you what they wrote, then later this afternoon after we've taught them how to cast, you tell *me* who you think said what."

Osborne sighed, wondering if the thimbleberry pie was worth it.

"Ready for the first one?"

"Please—and can we do this fast?"

" 'Since I don't golf, I need some outdoor sport I can do with clients.' "

"Okay . . . next?"

"Number two: 'I want to show my father that I can run a boat and catch a fish every bit as well as my brother might have. Get a little more respect.' "

"That's it?"

"Uh-huh."

"Hmmm." Never having raised a son, Osborne wasn't sure what to make of that one.

"Number three: 'The only reason I'm here is because someone else was afraid to come alone.'"

"Is that someone who even *wants* to fish?"

"See what I mean, Doc. I could be changing some lives—"

"Hit me with the last two. It's getting late."

"Number four is easy: 'I'm here because my friend said it would be good for our business.' You'll guess that one right away. But then . . . number five, Doc. . . ." Ray paused before he spoke, then enunciated each word with care: 'I need some way to avoid my husband . . . and I know he hates water.'

"Doc, you won't believe this girl. She is such a sweetheart. Very quiet, pretty as a forget-me-not. Can't be over a day over thirty. Can you . . . *imagine* . . . being so unhappy so early in a marriage?"

"That's too many clues, Ray—you're giving away the pie." By this time, Osborne knew the quiz had nothing to do with pie. Ray was looking for approval to misbehave.

"Seriously, Doc. What do you think of that last one?"

"I think you should mind your own business. An unhappy married woman? You're asking for trouble—you know that."

But Osborne had another thought that he kept to himself, one laced with guilt. How often had he gone fishing during his thirty-plus years of marriage just so he didn't have to listen to Mary Lee. A habit honed in desperation within three months of their wedding and two years short of *his* thirtieth birthday.

four

I'm not saying that all fly-fishing, yes, even bait-casting, is not a fine art . . . , but I do think that there are far too many people who are satisfied to accumulate tackle and terminology, rather than to fish."

—Negley Farson

Osborne ambled down the pine-needle path that passed for Ray's driveway. Nearing the small house trailer, he paused to take a long look around. Wow. No doubt the sunshine helped and the fresh air helped and the lush white pines gracing the sky overhead helped— but wow. Ray had outdone himself. Either that or a miracle had taken place.

Whether it was a heaven-sent downpour or a plain old garden hose, something had blasted the thatch of dead pine needles and dried leaves from the top of the rusting trailer—and splashed across the windows, too. They gleamed squeaky clean in the morning light.

Even the garish green muskie that Ray had painted across the front of the trailer seemed younger, livelier, *greener*. Osborne suspected a touch-up. The old "shark of the north" had been positioned so that its gaping jaws framed the entrance to the trailer. Today those raked spears glittered more ferociously than ever: thanks to a painterly piscatorial dental hygienist. By the name of Ray Pradt.

Backed in tight to one side of the trailer was the battered blue pickup, fenders peeling paint where rust had taken over. But even that managed to look spiffy, its leaping walleye hood ornament so polished and shiny it might have been made of sterling.

Osborne glanced at his watch as he strolled past the trailer towards the lake. It was not quite seven thirty, and the women weren't due until eight. But Ray must have been up since dawn. Over a dozen spinning rods rested side by side on the picnic table near the dock, price tags fluttering in the breezes. Five tackle boxes stood open on the table benches, their contents sorted into plastic trays as carefully as if they were spices in the pantry of a French chef.

At the sound of the screen door opening, Osborne turned. Ray descended from the jaws of the muskie, a happy grin on his face, a mug of hot coffee in one hand and his stuffed trout hat in the other. He was so freshly showered that the wet curls clustered across his forehead still glistened. Crisp khaki shorts and black Teva sandals exposed long, tanned, well-muscled legs and his shirt, sleeves rolled up, was freshly ironed to match the shorts.

"Hey, Doc. Whaddaya think?"

Walking over to the picnic table, Ray brushed at some invisible dirt before setting his hat down. Osborne could swear that trout was sporting new stuffing, and the silver on the lure crisscrossing its chest sparkled from a recent polish.

"Looks like you got everything under control," said

Osborne. He paused to study the contents of the tackle boxes. "Using some of your custom tackle?"

Ray liked to paint his own lures, deliberately reversing traditional color schemes. Since he caught more walleye and muskie than anybody else Osborne knew, he was probably on to something. But it was tough to say.

Could be the custom paint job, could be the poaching on private stocked lakes (Ray *never* said where a fish was caught nor was he expected to), or it could be the penchant for fishing out of season. Whatever it was, no one had better stats than Ray Pradt on the numbers of fish caught and mounted, fish caught and eaten, fish caught and released. Assuming you believed everything he said, which some folks found difficult. Not Osborne. He could always tell when his friend was exaggerating.

"Yeah, a couple of these are mine," said Ray, bending over one of the tackle boxes. "I want the ladies to try spoons, poppers, jerkbaits, crankbaits, surface baits. Some live bait, too—got plenty of minnows and leeches on the pontoon all ready to go. Speaking of which," he turned and pointed off to the left, "did you see the *We B Miss B Haven*?"

"No, I did not," said Osborne, noticing for the first time the surprise bobbing at the end of Ray's dock: a brand-spanking-new pontoon boat, the platform white with creamy leather seats and forest-green carpeting.

"Now, Ray, where the heck did you get this?" Osborne walked onto the dock. Ray followed. "This isn't yours. . . ."

"Heavens, no. This is forty thousand bucks' worth of

boat and motor. Borrowed it from the marina. Brusoe said if I can sell it to one of the gals, he'll give me a commission."

Ray stepped into the boat. "Look here," he flicked a switch near the steering wheel, "it's got a state-of-the-art locator/GPS system. You can see structure at the same time that you can pinpoint exactly where you are on the lake. Or zoom back and see where you are in the *county*, for God's sake. It's amazing.

"And here," he raised the lid of one of the seats, "LED lights to illuminate the livewells from the bottom up. Up here on the throttle—here's a button that'll raise and lower the prop without so much as a *whisper*. And that's one big outboard, too—you can pull a skier with this boat."

Osborne was beginning to think Ray wanted him along, not so much to help out but so he could show off these temporary toys of his. "The ladies will like the leather seats," he said, brushing his hand across one. It might be vinyl but it looked expensive.

"My ladies like *everything*," said Ray with a wink as he sipped from his mug.

"*Your* ladies, huh? You had a good first day, I take it."

"Great day. Doc, I'm on to something. I'll tell you, I'm a darn good teacher—and you won't believe the money these girls got to spend. I may not sell the boat, but you wait and see how many rods and all the tackle they'll buy—which they should if they want to fish with decent equipment. I'm not selling them anything they don't need, y'know."

"And you make a commission on everything, right?"

"You betcha."

"Well, who knows Ray, if you're having fun with the teaching. . . . Nice people, these women?"

Whatever his cash-flow crisis of the moment, Ray had standards. More than once he had refused to guide clients who were rude, too demanding, or just plain unpleasant.

He paused before answering. "Nice enough. Their answers as to why they signed up got me thinking though." His face tightened as he took a final sip of coffee then tossed the rest into the lake. Osborne caught the change of expression.

He shook his head as Ray walked back up to the trailer. It was going to be interesting to find out which of the five women was "pretty as a forget-me-not." Osborne was not going to be surprised if the poor husband who hated water found himself at risk of going overboard.

five

Beauty without grace is the hook without the bait.

—Ralph Waldo Emerson

Five minutes before eight, the first of Ray's students appeared on the horizon. She came by water and she came full-bore, not cutting the motor on the big outboard until the last second.

"Show-off," said Ray, hands thrust into his pockets as they watched the boat drift towards the dock. The high performance black Skeeter bassboat sparkled with the brilliance of a billion sequins: a dais befitting a lake queen and her entourage.

Make that *two* imperial images, thought Osborne, at the sight of the women on board. One sat watching from a rear seat—arms folded, legs crossed, eyes hidden beneath a wide-brimmed straw hat tied down with a scarf and dark glasses. Aloof, if not haughty. Not so the one behind the wheel: she was waving with all the enthusiasm of a Dairyland Princess in a Fourth of July parade.

And wearing a lemon meringue pie on her head. As the boat neared the dock, close enough for the driver to toss Ray a line, Osborne could see it wasn't a pie after all. The woman, who couldn't be more than five feet tall, had short hair, streaked blonde and swept back and up into a kind of pouf guaranteed to add at least two inches to her height.

"Doc," Ray ducked his head so his words wouldn't carry, "check out the name on this Skeeter." Along the side of the watercraft, custom-painted in silver edged with scarlet was one word: BOATOX.

"Ray, hoo-hoo! Good *moorning*!" As the woman continued to wave, she hollered at a decibel level six times louder than necessary.

"Ouch—is she always that loud?" asked Osborne, voice low under the throttle of the idling engine as Ray nursed the boat towards the dock.

"Yep, lives at the top of her voice."

As Ray stood by to help the driver up onto the dock, Osborne got a good look and all he could think was, "Please, Lord, don't do this to me."

Over the years, when he had encountered women like this, he did his best to avoid them. If they arrived in his office as potential patients, he'd waste no time referring them elsewhere. If they were friends of his late wife, their presence at a bridge game in his home would spur him out the door and into the boat no matter how bad the weather.

This particular version resembled an overripe raspberry. Her eyes were too bright, her lips too red, and her bosom too generous. The latter was pushing its way up and out of a sleeveless red blouse, shirttails knotted before meeting the waistband on her shorts, which were also red and way too tight. A fuzzy little pin with glittering eyes substituted for the most important button on her blouse. If it was intended to draw the eye to the valley of her cleavage, Osborne made sure not take the hint.

Looking everywhere except there, he estimated a dozen thin gold bracelets climbing her left arm and a scattering of rings across pudgy fingers tipped scarlet. Miniature diamonds outlined the lobe of one ear; at least as many pierced the other. No doubt she was fishing for more than just fish—but did she realize that if she fell in the lake, she might sink?

Even Ray noticed. As he gave her a hand up and out of the boat, he said, "What's that in your ear, Kitsy? Been tagged by the National Park Service?" With a mock grimace on her face, Kitsy punched him in the arm.

"*Hello* there," she said, pushing past Ray to thrust a hand at Osborne. "Dr. Osborne, remember me?" She had a grip so firm he could feel every ring. Returning the handshake with a silent wince, he struggled to place her face then gave up. He focused on the line of the jaw and the expanse of forehead—the two features least likely to have been surgically altered. "Well . . . now, I'm not sure. . . ."

"Kitsy Kelly! Dr. Osborne. Kitsy *McDonald* Kelly. You used to check my teeth every summer when I was a kid. Don't you remember? My mom would haul me into your office insisting I was eating so many marshmallows, every single one of my teeth would fall out." She hooted loudly.

"Of course, Kitsy. My apologies. How could I forget?"

He hadn't seen the woman since she was eleven—or was it twelve? Had to be twenty years ago, maybe longer. And this incarnation bore no resemblance to that sullen preteen. Certainly not those lips. Boatox, indeed.

Osborne was no stranger to the impact cosmetic surgery was having on dentistry. He may have retired from his practice but not his profession, not since Lew Ferris had been willing to trade time in the trout stream for his assistance with dental forensics.

Eager to maximize any opportunity to fish with the woman who had shown him how to cast a trout fly even as she hooked his heart, he made sure to keep current with national dental journals and stay active in the Wisconsin Dental Society, attending monthly meetings and seminars.

So he was familiar with Botox. Along with other advances in cosmetic surgery, it had become both a dollar sign and a favorite topic of conversation among the younger dentists. Lips fat with Botox signaled a patient likely to want her teeth whitened, straightened, capped, or crowned. Not to mention dental implants. It all translated to serious money. How much of that money was in Kitsy's mouth? He was happy not to know.

"Julia!" Kitsy turned to her friend, who was just stepping off the boat. "You won't believe who's here. Remember I told you I had that terrible crush on my dentist when I was a kid? This is the one!"

Kitsy turned back to Osborne, "Dr. Osborne—you still married?" Her eyes met his: bold and teasing. He gritted his teeth. If this continued all day, Ray would really, really owe him.

"Doc's widowed," said Ray, his tone soft and blunt enough to curb the conversation.

"Oh? Sorry to hear that," said Kitsy, not looking sorry at all. But she got the message. Waving a dismissive hand, she peered past Osborne, "Ooh," her voice ratcheted up six notches, "*loook* at all that good stuff. . . ." And off she scurried towards the picnic table.

"Nice to meet you, Dr. Osborne," said the second woman, removing her hat and sunglasses as she walked toward him, a ghost of a smile on a face so pale that Osborne hoped she had brought along some sunscreen.

"Julia Wendt." She extended a hand he was relieved to find free of metallic objects. But her grip was slight, fingers only. He wondered if she would have the strength to handle a spinning rod. Everything about her was fawn colored: her long-sleeved shirt, her trim pedal pushers, even her hair and eyes. She wasn't small. Her features were full and round, but she gave the effect of needing protection.

"So you know Kitsy from way back, I take it?" asked Julia, her voice so soft that Osborne had to lean in close to hear her better. So close he could smell her scent. It, too, was soft and lovely.

"Haven't seen her since she was a youngster," said Osborne. "I knew her mother's family and her parents, but I'm retired from my dental practice. I'm afraid I didn't recognize her. She's . . . changed."

"That is putting it mildly," said Julia with a laugh so pleasant, Osborne had to smile. "Kitsy is *addicted* to change."

"And how do you two know each other?" asked Osborne as they strolled down the dock and over toward the picnic table.

"Oh, we've been friends since our teens. Met at summer camp one year and now that we both live in Madison, every summer we try to get away for a week somewhere. Last year we went to Florence, Italy; this year we decided to come here."

"That's quite a contrast," said Osborne.

"Sure is," said Julia, raising her eyebrows and laughing. "But Kitsy has just finished decorating a beautiful, *beautiful* summer home she's built down the lake from her folks. She wanted to show it off. That, and that big honking boat of hers." Again, the pleasant peal of laughter.

She shook her head. "We almost didn't make it on time this morning. I was sure we'd get stuck in the channel on our way over."

"So you and Kitsy aren't staying at the big house?" said Osborne. "Well, I suppose it needs updating given it was built in the early nineteen hundreds. I'm sure the plumbing leaves something to be desired. These old lake lodges are so obsolete, must cost a fortune to update—"

"It's not that so much," said Julia. "She's . . . Kitsy loves it up here, but she's not exactly close to her folks." She hesitated. "You know, that's none of my business, and I shouldn't be saying anything."

"Families," said Osborne. "Can't live with 'em, can't live without 'em. You know what my daughters tell me is the definition of a dysfunctional family? More than one person."

Pleased with the ease with which he let her off the hook, Osborne excused himself to give Ray a hand. He watched her walk away towards the picnic table. He found her reserve attractive. Could she be Ray's forget-me-not? He made a mental note to check out her left hand.

six

Fish are strange creatures. They're even more unpre-dictable than women—and that's going some.

—R. V. Gadabout Gaddis

The red SUV that skidded into Ray's clearing just as he was handing Kitsy a spinning rod was so bright and shiny, from whitewalls to roof rack, that Osborne wouldn't have been surprised to learn it had been driven off a dealer's lot that morning. The behemoth stopped just short of a white birch, the engine idling while a muffled beat boomed from within.

Two heads were visible through the tinted win-dows—the silhouette on the driver's side enhanced with the drooping line of a cigarette. After a few sec-onds, the booming stopped. The driver opened her door and, jumping down from the high seat, paused to toss her cigarette into the sand and grind it down hard with her heel. Opening the rear door, she reached inside. Without waiting for her companion and clutching two plastic bottles, one in each hand, she hurried across the clearing towards the picnic table.

Osborne was relieved to see this student of the art of fishing was sensibly dressed in knee-length white cotton shorts, a blue-and-white striped T-shirt, and rubber-soled sandals. A tall, slender woman, her arms and legs were so thin he wondered if she was ill. A black leather fanny pack was slung low across her hips. Stopping for a moment, she tucked one bottle of Diet Coke under her left arm so she could shove her car keys into the fanny pack.

As she neared the table, Osborne had to make an effort not to stare. Her head, capped with a frizz of brown hair held back by a pair of sunglasses, was exceptionally small for her frame. The effect was exaggerated by broad cheekbones that tapered too quickly to her chin, giving her eyes the appearance of having been flattened. Her features had that hollow, weathered look that Osborne associated with people who chain-smoke, drink hard liquor, and watch too much television in the dark. Though she looked older, he guessed her to be in her late thirties.

Her eyes were vaguely familiar: small, dark, and darting like those of an inquisitive chipmunk. He knew those eyes. Osborne struggled to place her. He was as forgetful as the next fellow but rarely did he forget faces. How *did* he know those eyes? He knew he knew her from somewhere.

"Sure as hell we're not late are we? Ray?" The woman's voice was flat, accusing. "You said eight—right?" If a mistake had been made, it sure as hell wasn't hers.

"You're fine. Come on down," said Ray with a genial wave. "Where's that girlfriend of yours? Didn't she come today?"

As if Ray's words were the cue, the passenger door slammed and a heavyset woman in black shorts and a black T-shirt scurried around the SUV. "Don't start without me," she called, tripping as she ran.

"Carla . . . Barb," said Ray as the second woman neared the table, "I want you to meet Doctor Paul Osborne. Doc is my neighbor, my good friend, and a *superbly* experienced fisherman. He . . . has graciously consented . . ." Ray paused to emphasize the importance of Osborne's presence, "to help us out this morning. So, ladies, whatever he says . . . goes. Right, Doc?"

"Whatever you say, Ray," said Osborne, feeling a flush of embarrassment travel up his neck. He wasn't *that* good a fisherman.

From across the table, the new arrivals gave Osborne blank stares. He figured Carla to be the taller of the two; Barb, the pudgy one, perspiring as if she had been rushing since she was born. An attempt to push a mass of unruly reddish auburn hair into a wide barrette had failed—clumps still fell across her eyes. Freckles blanketed her ruddy face and all the exposed skin on her arms and legs. Wide hazel eyes, which might be her best feature under normal circumstances, looked worried.

"Sorry we're late," she said in a whiskey voice. At the sound of her friend's apology, annoyance flashed across Carla's face.

"Not a problem," said Ray, glancing at his watch. "We're waiting on one more person . . . I expect Molly any moment but, heck, let's get started." He turned to Osborne. "Doc, you help Carla and Barb select their rods—I'll work with Kitsy and Julia."

"Okeydoke," said Osborne, motioning to his team to

follow him. "Nice meeting you ladies," he said, extending a hand to each.

"C'mon, you know, Carla, Doc," said Ray, interrupting. "She's Darryl's daughter."

"Darryl's daughter . . . ," said Osborne, struggling to come up with a last name. He gave up: "Darryl who?"

He knew four men named Darryl: One was an orthodontist, one a retired military man who had been a patient, one his college roommate, and one was his late wife's brother. The woman in front of him was highly unlikely to be related to any of the four.

But this was typical of Ray who always assumed you knew everyone he did, which was impossible, as he knew or was known by everyone living within a hundred-mile radius of Loon Lake. Osborne was good on former patients and longtime friends and neighbors, even Mary Lee's bridge group, but short on Ray's circle of odd birds—many of whom *only* Ray knew.

"What do you mean 'Darryl who'?" asked Ray in disbelief. "What the heck—Wolniewicz was my right-hand man at the cemetery until he got himself a good job at the Newbold landfill last year. Doc, you'd know him if you saw him."

"Appreciate the family history," said Carla, eyes hostile.

"What?" asked Ray. "I'm sure Doc knows your father."

"Give it a rest, guy," said Carla, rolling her eyes. "I go to all the trouble of an eighty-thousand-dollar ad campaign for my new real estate office, and you have to go tell everyone my old man collects garbage."

Barb looked like she was going to cry, Kitsy raised an eyebrow at Julia, and Ray shrugged, "Garbage, schmarbage, I like your old man. Like him better'n some of the razzbonyas hanging around, and when it comes to fishing bluegills—"

"Oh, heck, I know who you mean," said Osborne, anxious to relieve the tension. "That fellow you fish bluegills with—right?"

"*Riiight,*" said Ray, drawing out the word.

Of course Osborne knew the man. Knew him and, like many folks in Loon Lake, felt sorry for him. Darryl Wolniewicz was one of those poor souls endowed with a face that terrified small children.

His skin was weathered a deep russet red, his beard resembled the back end of a porcupine, and his eyes had a way of fixating on you with an intense stare. A stare that was hard to avoid as the eyes were rimmed bright red. Life had not gone easy on Darryl.

From Osborne's perspective, it didn't contribute to his charm that he was missing his maxillary lateral incisors—his top two front teeth. Darryl's grin was a snarl.

Even adults found him unsettling to look at. Except for Ray Pradt.

In the winter when work was slow, Osborne would often catch a glimpse out his kitchen window of Darryl's rusted green van heading down to Ray's for a seventeenth cup of coffee. His neighbor had a fondness for the geezer that went beyond hiring him to help with the backhoe at the cemetery, shovel snow, or any of the other odd jobs with which he might need help. He was there to bail him out when Darryl committed his annual DUI.

And he had been as proud as a father when Darryl landed the trash-hauling job: "Doc, for the first time in his life the guy's got health insurance, a retirement plan, and a steady income. He deserves it—he's one hard worker and a good soul." Darryl also knew the best bluegill water, public and private, in the county. And he shared that knowledge with only one person: Ray's kindness paid off.

Before any more remarks could be made on Darryl's career path, a black Toyota Camry pulled up beside the SUV. A young woman stepped out, slung a backpack over one shoulder, and hurried towards them. Tall but small-boned, she gave the appearance of being long and light. She wore her straight, brown hair short and pushed back behind her ears to expose a clear, radiant face with wide, dark eyes that smiled the moment she saw Ray.

"Made it. Sorry, everyone. Had to drop my husband off at the paper. He took forever to get ready."

She wore no makeup, leaving her skin pale with a dusting of freckles across her nose. Like Barb and Carla, she was dressed appropriately in a long-sleeved white T-shirt, tan shorts of a sensible length, and black sandals.

Osborne felt his shoulders relax for the first time since Kitsy's arrival. At least Julia and Molly could be counted on to behave in reasonable ways. As far as the other three? Ray was moving deeper and deeper into the red.

Setting down her backpack, Molly pushed wisps of hair from her face as Ray said, "Meet the fifth member of our group, Doc—Molly O'Brien."

The girl's handshake was firm. "Nice to meet *you*, Doctor," she said, her voice low and confident. Then she brushed her hair back and took a deep breath. "And you? How are you this morning, Ray?" She thrust her hands into her pockets as she spoke.

"Lost all my marbles . . . making me absolutely marbleless," said Ray with a grin and a lift of his eyebrows.

"Oh, you," said Molly with a chortle. "Does this mean you'll torture us all day?"

"You betcha," said Ray, his eyes intent on hers. A smile bloomed across the girl's face as she glanced away.

That was all Osborne needed. The signs were as obvious as the ripples of a hungry fish at dusk. Molly O'Brien: Ray's forget-me-not.

seven

I want fish from fishing, but I want a great deal more than that, and getting it is not always dependent upon catching fish.

— Roderick Haig-Brown

Nudging the fishhook along so as not to rip a hole in his shirt, Osborne managed to wiggle it free from where it was lodged in the back of his right sleeve just below the shoulder. He was grateful it was early enough in the day that the women were still learning on #2 hooks with leeches and not one of Ray's treble-hook specials. That might have done some damage.

And he was glad it was Julia who had hooked him. Whether it was her lack of upper arm strength or enthusiasm—nothing about Julia's cast was life threatening. She did, however, prove Ray to be correct on one count: five women on one pontoon—all fishing for the first time—made life exciting. No doubt about it.

"Photo op!" said Ray, spotting Osborne's dilemma. He reached for the ancient Polaroid camera. "One human hooked—could be the largest catch of the day."

"Don't you dare," said Julia.

"Sorry," said Ray, "part of the package—you paid

for two photos. Shots of your first and your largest catches. Although you may get an extra—"

"Kitsy, get over here." Julia pulled her friend into camera range. "You got me into this. You're responsible for Dr. Osborne's emergency-room bills."

"I think I'll survive," said Osborne, as Ray leveled the camera at the three of them. Kitsy mimicked a look of astonishment while Julia, chagrined and embarrassed but sporting, held her rod so it was obvious her catch was a six-foot-three-inch man making an effort to look more distinguished than the average walleye.

Unlike the fish, he had a full head of black hair, silvered across the temples, quite a nice tan, and he was slim through the middle. And, thank goodness, his eyes were not plastered to the sides of his head, but well placed above the cheekbones that hinted of his Meteis heritage. At least that's what Osborne thought upon seeing the photo.

Julia studied the snapshot, eyes serious and bemused, before slipping it carefully into her back pocket and turning to Osborne for help selecting a fresh leech. To her credit, she insisted on impaling it herself.

Before boarding the pontoon earlier that morning, Ray had had the women test each of the spinning rods, which he had rigged with identical lures of the same weight. They were instructed to cast each one several times from the shore.

"Keep trying until you find the rod that feels like an extension of your arm, that has a flex that feels comfortable," said Ray. "Then hold on to it—that's your rod for the day."

The women pounced on the rods, each grabbing

several, then dashing down to the water's edge. "Remember what I said about those back casts," said Ray. "You don't want to hook each other." Happy and excited, they tried rod after rod.

The exercise was going well until Carla and Julia discovered they both liked the same rod. With that, all signs of camaraderie vanished: the rod in question gripped tight in Julia's right hand while the two women stood glaring at each another.

"This shouldn't be a problem," said Ray, stepping in to referee. "Don't I have another one of those? I thought I had two of each."

Osborne checked the rods on the picnic table. No duplicate there.

"I think I've got it," said Barb, walking up from the shore where she had been practicing her cast. "Here, Carla, you take mine."

"No," said Ray, "that's the one you wanted—isn't it, Barb?"

"Doesn't matter," said Barb. "I was thinking maybe I could try one of the muskie rods?"

"Those are for this afternoon," said Ray. Osborne shot him a look that was the equivalent of a kick in the butt. Couldn't he see poor Barb was doing her best to keep Carla happy? "Well . . . I guess that's okay," said Ray.

Finally they were on the boat, each woman outfitted with her own rod and a box of tackle. Puffy white clouds drifted overhead in a Dresden-blue sky as a light breeze threw shadows across the calm surface of the lake. Ray slowed to five mph as he finessed the pontoon through the shallow channel leading into Second Lake on the Loon Lake chain.

As the boat turned east, laser shards of sunlight sparked off the backs of turtles sunning on exposed boulders. A great blue heron lurked behind a petrified swirl of roots from a tree upended by some long-ago flatline wind.

Ray put a finger to his lips. "Watch," he said, cutting the motor to a low idle. He let the pontoon drift. The women were silent, all eyes on the elegant creature. "If we're lucky, we might see that heron bait a fish . . . watch now. . . ."

"What are we watching for?" whispered Molly.

"To see if he throws out a twig or an insect that he's caught. . . ."

"You're not serious," said Molly.

Ray shrugged.

"Birds do not have an intellect," said Molly, moving closer to Ray so she didn't have to speak too loudly. "Don't tell me you believe birds and animals think like we do—"

"What makes you think they don't?" said Ray. "You think fish aren't smart?"

Osborne smiled as they whispered. Well aware of the crafty muskies hunkered down on the lake bottom—not to mention the wily trout that eluded his trout fly, no matter how lightly he managed to drop it—this was one time he was on Ray's side.

The boat rocked gently, its seven passengers barely breathing. But the heron didn't move until the pontoon had drifted too near. Then it unfolded its origami wings and flew off in a huff.

"Oh, well, he wasn't having much luck anyhow," said Ray. "Probably needs fly-fishing lessons—on how to be less conspicuous. What do you think, Doc?"

"I think you should answer Molly's question. Do you believe that birds and animals have the capacity to think?"

"Better than some humans with whom I am familiar," said Ray. Carla rolled her flat eyes.

"Carla, Carla, *Carrrla*," said Ray with raised eyebrows and a wide smile, "I'm beginning to think," he waved an index finger at her, "that your sole purpose in life is to serve as a warning to others." The smile was his most charming, the one he used on clients he hoped never to see again.

Before Carla could utter a word, Ray gunned the motor.

The pontoon didn't stop until they had crossed the lake and were coasting along a loggy area known to be good for walleye. Spotting an underwater landmark that only he could see, Ray dropped the anchor and gave a nod to Osborne.

"Okeydoke, ladies," he said, "let's get started. I want you to try each of the lures that I've placed in that top shelf in your tackle boxes. If you need help, do not hesitate to ask. Give each one a good ten or fifteen minutes before you switch to another.

"When you've tried all of those, Doc has some live bait—minnows and leeches and a few nightcrawlers. Try those next."

Barb seized the muskie rod, sorted through the lower shelf of her tackle box, and slipped on a bucktail. Osborne watched as she grasped the rod with both hands, set her feet, brought both arms back, and let the lure fly high and long. She sure as hell was no beginner.

"Very nice," said Osborne, resisting the urge to ask

why she had lied. "You don't need lessons. But I suggest you try a minnow, Barb. It's early in the season and on a sunny, dead-calm day like today—with a cold front moving in, and the water warming—I've seen muskies go on a feeding spree. So try a minnow and cast in that direction."

He pointed to a weed bed off the left side of the pontoon.

Barb nodded and set down her rod to remove the bucktail. As Osborne reached into the minnow bucket for a six-incher, he asked in a low voice, "Why didn't you tell me you've done this before?"

Barb threw him a worried look. She checked to be sure Carla was at the far end of the boat and busy with her own casts before leaning towards Osborne to whisper, "I don't want her to know. Just say I'm a natural—something like that." Her eyes pleaded.

"Sure. But how long *have* you been fishing?"

"My dad taught me years ago. But I only ever fished muskies with him. These rods for bass and walleye—and all the lures? This is all new to me—"

"Dammit!" Molly plunked herself down on the seat beside them in exasperation. "Damn, damn, damn!" Ray was standing at the other end of the pontoon, his arms around Kitsy in attempt to smooth out her cast, so Osborne leaned over to see what Molly's problem was.

"Only a backlash—not the end of the world," said Osborne, taking hold of her rod, its reel snarled with fishing line. Molly looked like she was about to burst into tears. "Here's what we do when that happens. . . ." His fingers moving expertly, Osborne pulled at the line until the snarl was loosened, then reeled it in good and tight.

"There you go, Molly. All set to start over. You'll do it right next time. We all need a snarl or two to learn."

"Oh, gosh, I wish I could do that with my *life*," said Molly. Osborne looked down at the girl. She wasn't kidding. The expression in her eyes was so sad, all he could do was hand over the rod and pat her on the shoulder. He guessed her to be in her early thirties, around Erin's age, maybe younger. Too young for such a haunted look.

eight

One of the outstanding peculiarities of angling is its inexplicable capacity to inspire almost unanimous disagreement among its followers.

—John Alden Knight

Four walleye, three legal bluegill, one muskie "follow," and seven photo ops later, a break was called. Arms and shoulders were tired, but faces were happy. Even Julia, who had picked up her rod only once since landing her human. Carla, anointed "angler of the morning" by Ray, had landed two walleye (one over four pounds) and a good-sized bluegill. She was ecstatic.

"Man, oh man," she cackled after landing her third fish, "is this the sport for me or what? No wonder my old man wastes half his life in that damn boat of his. I could do this all day!" Her tense, dry laugh repeated itself like the hammering of a woodpecker. Again, it was vaguely familiar. Had she been a patient years ago? Maybe when she was in grade school? Osborne decided to check his files.

One of the smarter things he had done in life was find a hiding place for the oak file cabinets that held the paper records from his thirty years of practicing dentistry in Loon Lake. It was one of the few times he had lied to Mary Lee. First, he assured her that any records not needed by the acquiring dentist had been scrapped, and that the oak cabinets had been given to his former receptionist.

Then, while she was at one of her golf luncheons, he had enlisted Ray's help in moving the big oak cabinets, fading paper files and all, into a walled-off storage area at the back of his garage. He entered through a door off the small screened-in porch that he used for cleaning fish. Mary Lee never went there.

Over time he had added the leather-seated swivel chair from his office, a braided rug black with Mike's dog hair, a plug-in percolator he had owned since dental school, and a set of chipped and stained coffee mugs with the Marquette University logo.

Also, a floor lamp with a ripped shade that he had salvaged from his father's apartment after his death. The room was cozy with memories. He had only to pull open a drawer in one of those old cabinets, and a whiff of his office would take him back in time.

Unfold a record, and it was as if a former patient was in the dental chair beside him: their face, their smell, any dental problems they were having—and whether or not they paid their bill on time. After Mary Lee's death, he had spent an unconscionable amount of money heating the little room. He could have moved the cabinets indoors, but he loved having a door that opened into the past.

If he had ever seen Carla before—her dental records should not take too long to find.

• • •

"Shore lunch, ladies," said Ray, steering the pontoon towards an island slightly off the center of the fifth lake on the Loon chain. He docked the boat along a fallen log, which could serve as a makeshift dock. The women, ready for a bathroom break, hopped off the pontoon and scrambled up a hilly path to the picnic site.

Osborne followed. At the top of the hill, he was surprised to find Ray's camp stove set up in the fire pit, and a small cooler with a dozen bluegills on ice shaded by a stand of balsam. "Just in case we struck out," said Ray, walking up from behind, his arms full of supplies. "A friend of mine with a cabin across the way was nice enough to buzz that cooler and camp stove over for me earlier this morning."

"Well, we sure didn't strike out," said Osborne. "What happens next?"

"Gotta show these ladies how to clean their catch," said Ray. "I need you to unload the rest of our lunch while I set up. So if you'd go down to the pontoon and get that Loon Lake Market sack that's right by the driver's seat and my big green cooler . . . Kitsy? Carla? How 'bout you two giving Doc a hand, please?"

"Sure thing," said Kitsy, leading the way as the two women skipped down the path and across the log ahead of Osborne.

"I'll grab the sack," said Kitsy. Carla and Osborne bent their knees to grasp the handles of the large green cooler. It was heavy.

"Carla, can you manage okay?" asked Osborne. He glanced towards her only to find the woman staring at him, a sly, cruel smile in her eyes. And that's when he knew how he knew her.

• • •

The details of those drunken days after Mary Lee's death were lost to memory. All he could recall—though he didn't try hard—was the outline of a black, despairing year when he wasted too many nights crawling the underbelly of Loon Lake. For all its wild beauty on sunny days, under cover of darkness the northwoods can turn evil, a lair for lost souls. Somewhere, sometime, during those dark hours he must have known Carla.

An awful feeling churned his gut as he searched for something to say. But before he could utter a word, Carla had looked away—and smack into Kitsy's cleavage.

"What the hell?" asked Carla, eyes riveted. Kitsy was bent over, struggling to hoist the sack, which held three six-packs of soda. As she straightened up, she yanked her blouse back into place.

"Wait," said Carla, setting down her side of the cooler and stepping in front of Kitsy, "what *is* that creepy thing?" She pushed the top of the paper sack down to get a better look at the brooch, the only thing holding Kitsy's shirt closed at its critical juncture. "Is that a dead mouse?"

"I assure you it's not living," said Kitsy with a shift of her shoulders so Carla could have a better view. Anxious for anything that would divert Carla's attention from him, Osborne opted to look, too.

"Don't tell me you spent *money* on that?" asked Carla. The flattened body of a mouse appeared to be wearing the head of a small bird.

"I spent a *lot* of money on it," said Kitsy, raising her eyebrows to signify just how much. "I doubt you see much art in this neck of the woods but, trust me, this is *quite* extraordinary. It's sculpted from antique taxidermy collectibles by a very well-known artist in New York City. I *adore* it."

She shifted her shoulders again so Carla could view the pin from all angles. "Bought it when I was there last month. The artist had a special showing down in TriBeCa—she has an exhibit opening in August out in L.A. if you're interested, and you can see her stuff on the Internet. Isn't it cool?"

"It's dead," said Carla, eyes still glued to Kitsy's shirt as if she expected the pin to make a move at any moment.

"Like I said—it's art," said Kitsy. "A-R-T. Art."

"Give me one good reason you would pay money for something like that . . . dead thing," said Carla.

Kitsy closed her eyes in concentration, then opened them as she said, "Because it is *so* wrong—and yet so right. And, while I don't expect you to understand, to me it speaks of the *dichotomy* of life."

Carla gave her a dim eye. "*Ookay.*"

At that moment, they heard a beeping. All three looked down at their feet. The sound appeared to be coming from a red leather backpack leaning against one of the seats containing a livewell.

"That's mine," said Kitsy, hurriedly setting down the paper sack as she knelt to unzip the backpack. She pulled out a cell phone cased in black Gore-Tex.

"Hello?" She grinned at Osborne and Carla as she listened, then turned to point back behind them. On the hill above the fire pit stood a female figure silhouetted against the bright sky. "You're kidding . . . *quilted* tissue?" said Kitsy. Covering the mouthpiece, she said, "It's Julia." She listened again, then clicked it off.

"Carla, Julia found us a latrine on the other side of the island—with all the comforts of home."

"I can't believe your cell phone works here," said Carla. "Mine sure doesn't. Just tried it a few minutes ago."

"This is a walkie-talkie—with a built-in GPS system," said Kitsy, holding the unit out towards Carla.

"That's not a bad idea," said Osborne. "Cell phones aren't much good when you've got heavy leaf cover and thick stands of pine like this. You've got a much better chance in the woods with a radio. Both Ray and I use walkie-talkies when we're deer hunting. But, Kitsy, I don't care what they told you when you bought it—don't bet your life on the GPS. If a cell-phone satellite signal is blocked, you better believe you'll have the same problem with that GPS signal."

"Still . . ." said Carla, turning the device over and testing its weight before handing it back to Kitsy. "Hell of a better investment than that pin of yours. Where did you get this?"

"The sporting goods shop in Loon Lake. Ralph's," said Kitsy, shoving the unit back into her pack. As she did so, a small leather-tooled holster, the same red as the backpack, bounced onto the floor at Carla's feet. The holster held a small pistol.

"Whoa!" said Carla, taking a quick step back. "I sincerely hope that's not loaded."

"'Course not," said Kitsy. "I'm not stupid."

Carla looked doubtful as Kitsy shoved the holster deep into her backpack.

"Whatever you say," said Carla. "But before you

spend a lot of money on another dead mouse, why don't you just shoot it yourself." And she cackled.

Osborne grasped one handle of the cooler, Carla the other. He took care all the way up to the fire pit not to look her way.

nine

Now, who can solve my problem,
And grant my lifelong wish,
Are fishermen all big liars?
Or do only liars fish?

—Theodore Sharp

"Okay, ladies, pay attention now—" said Ray with a wave of his knife. The words were unnecessary: his students were transfixed.

"To remove the gills on this bluegill, you start with a cut here at the throat connection, then slip your knife along both sides of the arch . . . and voilà! See how easy the gills pull out? Now insert the point of your knife into the vent right here . . . and run that tip *riight* up to the gills—but be careful you don't penetrate the intestines. Like this . . . then push your thumb into the throat . . . and pull the gills and guts toward the tail. Just . . . like . . . that."

Ray had already demonstrated his "soup spoon" scaling method and dropped two sticks of butter into the frying pan. At the moment, the butter was just starting to froth over a low flame on the camp stove.

"Will you do another one?" asked Carla. "Like show

us how you fillet? How 'bout that big walleye that I caught?"

As Ray reached for the walleye, the women groaned but their eyes never left his hands. Who knew evisceration could be so fascinating?

"First, with the walleye, we go for the gold," said Ray. "We want the cheeks, and they are . . . a *delllicaacy*. . . ." Piercing two soft spots near the head, he popped out the coin-shaped nuggets and with a flick of the blade slipped off the skin. The disks glistened on the waxed paper.

"Those, Carla," said Ray, "are your reward. You will never forget your first walleye cheeks." Carla appeared to melt. For the first time that day, she dropped her hard-bitten attitude to grin like a little kid.

Keeping up a steady banter, Ray worked his knife through the fish until boneless, skinless fillets of blue-gray walleye, exquisite as marble, slid into the melted butter.

"I'll never be able to do that," said Molly with a sigh. Osborne had to agree. He never tired of watching Ray whip through his limit or more of fish caught fresh just hours before. In his lifetime, he'd known maybe one or two men who, like his neighbor, could wield the fillet knife as if it were an artist's tool: deft, quick, and accurate.

With the fish sautéed and every morsel devoured, the homemade potato salad long gone, and only two of a dozen "homemade-from-scratch" brownies remaining, Ray poured fresh-perked coffee from his battered pot into foam cups. The women leaned against logs set back from the fire pit—legs extended, hats off, faces lifted to the sun. Even Osborne, who had managed to find a spot out of Carla's line of sight, was relaxed.

"Molly," said Julia, as Ray handed her a cup of coffee, "you haven't told us about your new husband."

"Right," said Molly, holding her cup out for a refill. "And I haven't asked about yours either—have I." She smiled as she sipped the hot coffee, but her eyes were serious.

"I don't have one," said Julia. "An ex, of course, but that doesn't count. So who is he?"

"Do we have to talk about this?" asked Molly. She looked around for support but all eyes were interested, waiting. She shrugged and said, "Jerry O'Brien. He just retired as publisher of the Loon Lake newspaper. He was a friend of my dad's."

"You married a friend of your old man's?" asked Carla. "Why would you do that? I know that guy. My god, he must be thirty years older'n you."

"Thirty-one," said Molly. "Seemed like a good idea at the time." She took a deep swallow of her coffee and tossed the rest into the bushes. Then she stood up, dusted off her hands, and started up the path towards the latrine.

"Wait a minute," said Carla, the sly look creeping across her face. "You gotta tell us—what's it like, you know, with an old geezer?" Her mouth twitched.

Molly turned to look straight at her. No smile this time. "I wouldn't know. He had prostate surgery just before we got together. Any more questions burning on your brain?" Carla waved off the challenge with a flutter of her hand.

"Score one for Molly," said Barb with a snort and a laugh—until she caught a glower from Carla.

"Whoa," said Kitsy when Molly was out of earshot. "Whoa."

She spoke for everyone, including Osborne. Jerry O'Brien had been a patient of his up until Osborne's retirement. Given the wear on his teeth, he had to be at least sixty-five. More memorable than the man's mouth was the awful cologne he wore. After every appointment, Osborne's dental assistant would have to open the office windows—even on a subzero winter day.

Molly married to Jerry O'Brien? Osborne was stunned.

"How many men does it take to screw in a lightbulb?" asked Carla, ready to change the subject.

"Excuse me," said Ray standing up, "I believe the time has arrived for me to see a man about a dog." Osborne resisted the urge to follow him down the path toward the lake.

"You tell us," said Kitsy. "You look like you know a lot about men."

"One. He just holds it and waits for the world to revolve around him." Carla cackled at her own joke.

"Now wait a minute," said Kitsy. "That is absolutely not true of our fishing guru. Ray doesn't strike me as the self-centered type." She looked around at the other women.

"I agree," said Barb. "Doc isn't either." She shot Osborne a quick glance, shy but grateful.

As if any remark by Barb bored her, Carla rolled her

eyes, unzipped her fanny pack, and pulled out a cell phone.

Punching in numbers, Carla turned away from the group, only to turn back after a few seconds and snap the phone shut. "Damn, still doesn't work," she said.

"Carla," Ray asked, trudging up the path just as she was putting her phone away, "didn't I tell you no cell phones allowed when you're fishing with me? Frightens the fish, doncha know?"

"How much you want for the pontoon?" asked Carla, ignoring his remark. "It's for sale, right?"

"Thirty-seven thousand," said Ray, "includes the trailer."

"Any discount for cash?"

"Carla, good heavens. What business are you in?" asked Molly as she returned to toss her paper plate into the trash bag that Osborne was holding. "Drugs?" At the look on Carla's face, she raised a hand—"Just kidding." But she couldn't resist a smirk, and Osborne didn't blame her.

"Real estate," said Carla. "Opened my own office about six months ago."

"Oh, really," said Molly as she sat down on a log. "You must be doing very well."

"I do okay," said Carla.

"Not just okay," said Barb, "we're doin' *great*. Carla got us this client. This big foundation that wants to buy and sell all this land. . . . Man, we are making money hand over fist. Just listed a big chunk of lake frontage over on Secret Lake."

The alarm on Carla's face went unnoticed by Barb, who had her back to her.

"What do you mean?" asked Kitsy, sputtering into

her coffee. "That's my lake. My family owns all the land surrounding that lake. Like who listed anything over there?"

"The Conservation Foundation is buying it from a Mr. Kelly for us to sell on his behalf," said Barb, still unaware of Carla's expression. "And we already have a buyer. So we make money on both sides. Very cool."

"Edward Kelly is my father," said Kitsy. "He can't possibly have listed property with you—"

"I have the name right, don't I?" Barb turned to face Carla. Too late, she got the message and froze.

"Well, he did," said Carla. "Three hundred acres. You seem surprised, but it's only a smidgen of everything your family owns over there."

"That's not it," said Kitsy, color rising in her face. "The land is in my mother's name. Dad can't do that."

"That's not what the records show," said Carla, her voice calm.

"Hey, everyone," said Julia, jumping to her feet. "That's enough business talk. We're here to fish. Now a big thank-you to Ray for a delicious shore lunch. What do we say?" She raised her arms as if directing an orchestra.

Everyone looked up in surprise. This was more animated than she had been all day.

"Thank you, Ray," they chorused. Even Kitsy, despite the worry clouding her eyes.

Ray beamed. "Ladies, ladies. Bread feeds the body, flowers the soul. Now back on the pontoon, everyone."

ten

*Then do you mean that I have got to go on catching these
damned two-and-a-half pounders at this corner forever
and ever?*
The keeper nodded.
"Hell," said Mr. Castwell.
"Yes," said his keeper.

—G.E.M. Skues

"Ray, how much longer?"

Dusk was falling, and Osborne was anxious. He and
Lew had agreed to meet at nine for an hour of fishing,
and it was already eight fifteen. It was obvious, too,
that the women were tiring. They had fished all afternoon until five thirty when Ray docked the pontoon at
Watersides, a small resort on Third Lake renowned for
its cozy dining room and excellent food.

"Burgers, fries, Leinies all around—except for me,
I'd like a Coke, and ginger ale for the good dentist
here," said Ray. Only Julia resisted, requesting water
not beer. Then it was back on the pontoon for one final
hour—or so Osborne had thought—of evening fishing. But dusk into dark was Ray's favorite time to fish,

and as the pontoon headed toward Fifth Lake Osborne realized their earlier agreement was being finessed.

"Ray . . ." he said, pointing at his watch for the umpteenth time and not a little irritated that he would have no time to shower and shave before Lew arrived. "I thought we agreed I would help out until six—it's way past that now. Ray?"

"Okay, okay, Doc, I hear you," said Ray from where he stood with his arms around Molly, helping her with a muskie rod. "Let's try one last cast, Molly," he said. "Remember what I told you. No reason to wrestle the rod—just aim for the horizon and let that Jitterbug fly. Good . . . that's it . . . great!

"And from now on, when you're fishing, what do you say to yourself? Repeat after me: *Perfect is the enemy of good enough.* Memorize that, let your lure fly, and I promise you will catch fish." Molly grinned, repeated his words and, both hands gripping her rod, let fly a long, smooth cast. Ray beamed, Molly glowed, and Osborne checked his watch.

"Ray. . . ." Osborne twisted his face into the grimace he used on Mike when the dog misbehaved. That got Ray's attention. He gave a sad little shrug, making it clear Osborne was the party pooper of the day, and sat down to turn the ignition key.

Twenty minutes later, as they entered the channel returning them to First Lake, the western sky greeted them with a watercolor vista: streaks and swirls of lavender and rose tipped gold by the setting sun. The women oohed and aahed and begged Osborne to take one more photo.

They crowded together behind Ray, arms linked, the

vibrant sky their backdrop. Checking the exposure and the angle, he made sure the sun didn't turn them into silhouettes. Then everyone settled down to bask in the final moments of the cruise, expressions of bliss on their faces. Ray couldn't have paid for a better finale to his first "Fishing for Girls."

As they rounded the last set of channel markers, a cell phone rang. Carla had the grace to look to Ray for permission before unzipping her fanny pack.

"Go ahead," he said, waving his hand, "we're done for the day."

She pulled it out and listened. "Are you shitting me—when did they call?" Carla jumped to her feet. "What? *They came into the office?*" A string of expletives filled the air. She slammed the phone shut and turned to Barb. "What the hell dumb thing did you do? Godammit."

"What—" asked Barb, "what are you talking about?"

"That was Tomisue at the office. The IRS *dropped in* this afternoon. They're doing an audit."

"I—I can't imagine why. . . ." Even the sunburn drained from Barb's face.

"You can't imagine why," mimicked Carla, shaking the phone at her.

"Ladies, that's enough," said Ray. But the day was robbed. Its golden haze of easy chatter, pleasant fatigue, and simple happiness shattered. Kitsy, Julia, and Molly averted their eyes. Barb sat with her shoulders hunched, trembling. The pontoon moved with a whisper over the water and no one said a word.

As they reached the end of the channel, Ray glanced

over at Carla. "Hey, Carla," he asked, "you know what they call an IRS audit, doncha?"

"Not interested," said Carla. She sat at the back end of the pontoon, arms folded tight against her chest, one leg crossed over the other, right foot pumping up and down.

Osborne, resting his forearms on his knees, reached his hands up to rub his eyes. He never knew which was worse: Ray's jokes or his timing. He also knew there was no stopping the guy.

"An autopsy—without benefit of death."

With the exception of Barb, the other women chuckled softly. Osborne pressed his fingers against his eyelids to keep from doing the same. After a few beats of silence, he dared to look up.

Carla's jaw was set. "So if I stop by tomorrow morning—will you let me have this pontoon?"

"Sure," said Ray, taken aback. "But—you really want to pay cash?"

"Yeah, I want to pay goddam cash. But I'll need you to help me with some arrangements. We'll talk about it tomorrow."

More moments of silence as the pontoon picked up speed on the lake. Ray reached down for his trout hat and set it on his head, adjusting it until he was satisfied the angle was just right. In Ray's world, no matter how distressing current events, arrivals and departures demand ritual.

"Speaking of cash, Ray," Kitsy asked, "how much will you take for that hat? I have *got* to have it."

"Not for sale."

"A hundred dollars."

"Nope."

"Five hundred . . . okay, okay, final offer—*one thousand dollars.*"

"She spends that much on dead mice," said Carla. "I'd take it."

Ray just grinned. "You can buy my tackle, my boat, my house trailer even—but you cannot buy my hat."

Kitsy gave him a teasing look. "We'll see. . . . Say, Carla," said Kitsy, bending over to pull a notebook out of her backpack, "before I forget—what's your office number if I want to get in touch with you on that property situation?"

"Julia's got it."

"*Julia's* got your phone number?" asked Kitsy.

"Yes, I asked her for it a while ago—I knew you would want it," said Julia with a half-smile on her face. As she spoke, Osborne saw Carla dart a look at Barb. No annoyance this time. Relief.

As the pontoon rounded the bend, Ray looked back at Osborne. "Hey, Doc," he said, pointing at the shoreline, "Someone's waving at us from your place. Hold on, ladies!" He gunned the engine.

"If it's Lew, she's early," shouted Osborne. Ray bypassed his own dock and headed straight for Osborne's. It was Lew, but she wasn't dressed for fishing. She was still in uniform, and she wasn't smiling.

eleven

I am not a lady fly fisher; I am a fly fisherman.

—Lady Beaverkill (Mrs. Louise Miller)

"Something wrong?" asked Osborne as Ray cut the engine to let the pontoon drift toward the dock.

Had something happened to Erin, or one of his grandchildren? Had there been a call from Chicago where Mallory was in Northwestern University's MBA program? In grad school and in AA—at least he hoped she was still in AA. That was one struggle he knew too well. Osborne held his breath.

"I need your boat, Doc," said Lew, keeping her voice low as he jumped off the pontoon. "Take me at least an hour to catch up with Roger and haul that department inboard of ours out of the garage. Hope you don't mind."

Hardly. That was good news. Osborne exhaled.

This was not the first time she had asked to use his boat. With three hundred lakes located within five miles of Loon Lake, it didn't make sense for the police department to keep their boat moored anywhere except on land. Further complicating water access were the locations of public landings—not always easy to reach, not to mention deep enough to handle the propeller. Getting the police boat in water was not easy and never fast.

"Of course not. Need help?"

"If you've got time, I would appreciate it."

Osborne resisted the urge to say, "Are you kidding?" Instead, he segued into an emotional state of heightened awareness tempered with happiness. The sight of her never ceased to hijack his heart—a heart, he admitted only to himself, that was of a sixteen-year-old trapped in the body of a middle-aged man.

Though his crush on the Loon Lake Chief of Police was well into its second year, he had known her longer. During his years as one of only three dentists in their small town, its population recently skyrocketing to 3,412, she made appointments twice a year, along with her young son and daughter, for a checkup and a cleaning.

Her teeth were excellent: small and hard in a jaw square enough to hold four wisdom teeth easily. A near-perfect bite and only two fillings.

Those were difficult years for Lew. A single mother, she worked at the paper mill and paid her dental bill in small monthly increments. But she always paid it off before her next appointment, which was more than he could say of too many of his more well-to-do patients.

But he sold his practice right around the time that Lew Ferris had joined the Loon Lake Police Department. They might never have gotten together if he hadn't decided to clean his garage one Saturday morning and stumbled onto a fly rod he had hidden away so well it was forgotten.

Years earlier, at the urging of a fellow dentist who
had been an expert in the trout stream, he had wanted
to try fly-fishing. He'd bought a couple books, even in-
vested in basic equipment. But Mary Lee, a chronic
complainer about the time he already spent in the boat
pursuing muskie, walleye, and panfish, nixed the idea.
The prospect of one more way for him to escape to
water infuriated her. And so, bowing to the wifely ha-
rangue, he gave up after one try.

Two years after her death, he decided to reorganize
the garage the way *he* would like it—and came upon
the gear from that aborted attempt. The bamboo rod appeared to be in excellent condition, as did the reel and
the trout flies.

He decided to take one lesson in casting before selling the equipment. Just to be sure that selling was the
right idea. To his great surprise, the instructor referred
to him by Ralph Steadman, who ran Ralph's Sporting
Goods, was a woman. And since their first hours in the
trout stream, he had found himself angling for more
time with her—in water, on water, near water. Anywhere.

It wasn't easy. Unlike Mary Lee and her bridge part-
ners, Lewellyn Ferris didn't need a man to bait her
hook or tie on her trout fly, carry her equipment or give
her a hand in the current. She was quite capable of
doing it all herself. She *wanted* to do it herself.

But the one thing he was pleased to discover that she
didn't have, following her promotion to Chief of the
Loon Lake Police Department, was a reliable forensic
odontologist. Budget restraints statewide hammered
law enforcement staffing. Not even the Wausau Crime
Lab, sixty miles away and Loon Lake's primary re-

source in the event of a serious crime, had a full-time forensic dentist.

Osborne, who prided himself on eyes sharp enough to spot a muskie twenty feet away in dark water, saw opportunity: Every corpse needs a reliable ID, and no ID is more reliable than teeth. And so it was that he honed his forensic skills—tools to trade for time in the water with a woman who made him feel young again.

Ray's pontoon lingered at the end of Osborne's dock, his neighbor waiting to be sure help wasn't needed. Lew waved him off. "Catch up with you later, Ray," she said, her tone pleasant but brusque. He got the message and gunned the pontoon into a wide, sweeping arc back towards his place.

"Oh—you've got everything ready to go, I see," said Osborne. A quick glance into his Alumacraft showed the heavy gas tank had been carried down from his garage and hooked up. Even the boat plug was in.

"You've been waiting long?" He gave her a hand into the boat before spinning the wheel to lower it from the shore station.

"Less than ten minutes. Long enough to see you weren't around. If you hadn't gotten back, I would've gone ahead, Doc. Didn't think you would mind. Had a call on a possible break-in about twenty minutes ago—up on Secret Lake. And you know how long it takes to drive back in there."

"Has to be the McDonald estate," said Osborne, yanking the cord on his Mercury 9.9 outboard. The engine purred into action. "The old place or the new one?"

"I didn't know there was a new one."

"The owner's daughter is one of the women on

Ray's pontoon over there," said Osborne as they sped past Ray's dock. He had to shout over the engine noise. "Maybe we should swing back? Ask Ray if we can borrow that pontoon—it's faster."

Lew looked back to where the women were just getting off the pontoon, each with an armful of gear.

"No, keep going, Doc. That pontoon might be too wide. I know we can get this boat up that channel. Very likely this is a false alarm, and why worry the family."

"You're right."

When they reached the narrow channel, so well hidden behind a peninsula of tamarack that few, besides Loon Lake natives, knew it existed, he lowered the engine speed and hitched the little outboard up two notches, just deep enough to keep them moving forward. The channel was tricky—shallow in spots and studded with deadheads.

"It'll take us six or seven minutes to reach Secret Lake," said Osborne. "I haven't been up here in a few years but Kitsy, the daughter I mentioned, brought her boat down here earlier today, so I'm sure it's navigable. You think someone may have broken into the big house? That's gated property, Lew."

"All I know is the security system went off, and no one answers at the house," said Lew. "And if there is a problem, I may have to scratch our plans for tonight. So let's hope not." She lifted her face to the north. "Feel that wind, Doc. The front is moving in. Doggone! Keep your fingers crossed all we've got is a pesky racoon."

He watched her as she spoke, the fading sunset infusing her tanned, open face with a warm glow. She wore no makeup, and her dark brown curls crowded haphazardly around her face. If Lew had a flaw, it was lack of pretense. She was direct, honest, and blessed with a frank, funny laugh that could burst out when you least expected it. Some men he knew found her a little too tough, a little too bright. He found her fun.

And he loved the curves of her body, to feel her breasts against him. Not a slim woman, Lew was sturdy: muscled and fit. The opposite of his late wife who could never have carried the gas tank for the outboard, much less considered doing so. Lew had more in common with his fishing buddies: she was the first woman he had ever known to be as good a friend as she was a lover.

His daughters had taken to looking at him with a question in their eyes. A question he couldn't answer. Or maybe it was one he was afraid to ask. Maybe he was afraid to ask because he knew the answer. Maybe he knew that if he asked the question, the answer would be that like the wild trout she loved to catch and release, Lewellyn, too, needed to be free.

twelve

When you visit strange waters go alone. . . . Play the game out with the stream . . . then all you learn will be your very own.

—R. Sinclair Carr

"**One** thing worries me, Doc," said Lew as Osborne maneuvered the boat through the twisting waterway. "We haven't had any false alarms from this place—so there could be a problem. Erin said you know the family?"

"Not well. Hope and Ed Kelly, her husband, were summer patients over the years," said Osborne. "Hope was the senior McDonalds' only child—her father inherited the land and built the big house. The family made their money in paper pulp years ago. Hope's daughter, Kitsy, is one of the women who signed up for Ray's fishing clinic today. She and a friend of hers from Madison—Julia Wendt."

"Anyone else there I might know?"

"Carla Wolniewicz?"

"Carla Wolniewicz," said Lew, cocking her head as if she hadn't heard right. "You're kidding. There's a strange one to show up for a fishing clinic. I thought she spent her waking hours at the casino—or in the bars." Osborne winced at that comment.

"To the contrary," he said. "Sounds like she runs a successful real estate business. Although she ended the day pretty upset—got news she's being audited by the IRS."

"Now that fits the Carla I know," said Lew. "Couldn't walk a straight line drunk or sober. I'm sure the IRS has good reason—and if I sound prejudiced, Doc, I am. She was there the night my son was killed. It was her boyfriend at the time who knifed him."

Lew stared off into the tamarack, now black against the night sky, her face drawn with sadness the way it always was when she remembered that night.

Osborne knew the story: how her son, who took after his father whom Lew divorced right after the boy was born, ran with a rough crowd, ended up in a bar fight, and was killed. He was only fifteen. The kid who knifed him got off with probation, thanks to an uncle who was a hunting buddy of the county judge.

The loss of her son galvanized Lew, prompting her to study law enforcement, complete a college degree, and join the Loon Lake Police Department as their first female patrol officer. Once on the force, she demonstrated a fierce sense of fair play, which may be why four years later she was named chief.

"Yep, I know Carla too well. Her father—she's Darryl Wolniewicz's kid, y'know. He's a sad soul. Heavy drinker. Used to get beat up by his wife before she ran off. Left Carla with him. Doesn't he help Ray out at the cemetery?"

"Not any longer. That Carla," Osborne said, shaking

his head as he thought back over the afternoon, "she's one tough cookie. Ever strike you she's a bully?"

Lew snorted. "That was her mother. Tell you something else about Carla—so happens she was working at the mill credit union a few years back. We heard rumors of some fancy footwork with the bookkeeping over there. No charges were ever filed, and I don't know that they ever proved anything, but she left under a cloud."

The channel widened as they were nearing the end. Osborne lowered the outboard back into the water. He revved the engine, letting the boat speed across the modest-sized lake toward the McDonald estate, which anchored the far end and was barely visible in the fading light.

"Hey, Doc, check out that quaint little twenty-thousand-square-foot retreat over to the right," said Lew. "Must be the daughter's place."

Located midway between the mansion and the channel was a log home typical of the ones being built by people from the cities with too much to spend. Lights blazed from all the windows, making it easy to see the house was three stories high and windowed all around, top to bottom. Outdoor lighting illuminated a mammoth fake rock chimney—and three decks.

On one of the decks stood a figure in white busy over an outdoor grill.

"Hired help?" asked Lew.

"Wouldn't surprise me," said Osborne.

"Jeez Louise," said Lew, and they exchanged a look that said it all: life in the northwoods is supposed to be about simplicity. Leave the manicured lawn, the household help, the social calendar behind. Some folks just don't have that talent—or perhaps they can't bear to be alone.

"Now *that* is downright disappointing." Lew waggled a finger towards the shoreline where tons of boulders had been dumped and wedged to form a wall the width of the lot: expensive décor for the lakeshore guaranteed to please the eye even as it destroyed natural habitat for fish and wildlife. The very habitat that would have seduced Great-Grandfather McDonald into buying the property in the first place.

Less than a minute later, their boat pulled up to the U-shaped dock fronting the old estate. The dock was unlit, shadowed by white pines bordering the property, though solar-powered lanterns sunk low to the ground illuminated a stone path leading past a wooden gazebo and up across the lawn to a wide deck. A pontoon boat, moored to one side and covered with a tarp, rocked in the wake of the Alumacraft.

Lew jumped onto the dock while Osborne tied off the boat.

"Might be a good idea to stay behind me in the shadows," said Lew, hunkering down and indicating a route along the right side of the yard that was well shadowed by shrubbery. "Until we know who's up there . . ." She had her Sig Sauer out of its holster. He had a flashlight—a heavy flashlight.

Osborne followed her, hoping he wouldn't trip on anything in the dark. A chandelier glowed low and intimate in a room opening off the left end of the deck. At the steps leading up onto the deck, Lew paused, motioning for Osborne to do the same—but there was no movement or sound from within.

"Stay here," she said with a whisper, then slipped up

onto the deck without making a sound and crossed to the nearest window. She peered in. She knocked lightly and waited. Nothing. "Looks like a porch—no sign of anyone."

She waved him forward as she walked along the deck toward the French doors and tried the latch. Locked. She knocked on the doorframe. The lighted room was to their left, but still no sound or movement. Osborne came up behind her.

"I see someone sitting at that table, but they're not responding to my knock," said Lew.

"Could be they're hard of hearing?" asked Osborne. "Hope is in her seventies." Lew moved down the deck for a better view of the seated figure.

"Oh . . ." she stepped back. "Not good, Doc."

Osborne stepped forward. Nope, no fishing tonight.

The sound of a motorboat drifted up from the lake. Lew and Osborne turned towards the sound, waiting, but it stopped before reaching the dock below. From across the water, they could hear voices, happy and relaxed.

"That'll be Kitsy and Julia," said Osborne. "You want me to say something?"

"Not yet. Not until we know more."

After checking the perimeter of the house only to find every door locked, Lew stationed herself in the center of the lakeside lawn, tried her cell phone, then snapped it shut. "No signal. How far down the driveway to the road—any idea?"

"Maybe a third of a mile at the most. Once we reach the road, there's a house right across the way," said Osborne. "A woman friend of Ray's lives there. Want to see if someone's home? Use her phone? Be faster than taking my boat back."

"Worth a try. This was dumb of me to come by boat. At least my cruiser has a radio."

"Take it easy, Lew, you can see enough through that window—another half hour is not going to make a difference."

A young girl came to the screen door of the homely little cabin, which couldn't have held more than two bedrooms. The look on her face when she saw Lew in uniform with her badge and her gun was one Osborne hoped never to see in a child's eyes again: utter terror.

"Don't worry, hon. I just need to use your phone," said Lew. "Is your mother home?"

After opening the screen door for them to enter, the girl backed away, speechless. "Really, don't be afraid," said Lew, her eyes dark with kindness. The girl was shaking. "This has nothing to do with you. Is your mom home? I'd like permission to use your telephone is all."

"She's . . . she's at work," the girl managed to say, then pointed to a cordless phone resting on the kitchen counter. Lew reached for it, then stepped back outside as she punched in the number for Marlene on the switchboard.

Osborne waited just inside the door. He was concerned for the girl who sat down in a chair at the nearby kitchen table. The room was worn but tidy. A boy, younger than the girl, walked in and stood behind her, his eyes wide with worry. Glancing around, Osborne saw two pairs of sneakers set neatly to one side of the refrigerator. They were wet.

"Excuse me, kids," he said, thinking his presence was frightening the two children even more. "We'll be gone in a minute." He stepped outside.

Lew kept her voice low as she spoke. "Marlene, call the security office over in Rhinelander. Be sure they've turned off the alarm system off from their end—very likely it's zoned. If they can't do that, tell them I want someone out here immediately. I'll hold while you call. . . ." She covered the receiver while she waited.

"Let's hope we don't have to wait an hour for security to show up, Doc. . . . Oh, okay, what is it?" Lew jotted down a number on the small notepad she had pulled from her shirt pocket. "Oh, really? That's good news.

"Will you please give Todd a call and apologize for me—but he's going to have to come back on duty tonight. I need him out here ASAP—"

"Lew," said Osborne.

She paused. "Hold on, Marlene—what is it, Doc?"

"Sorry to interrupt," said Osborne, "but why don't you have Todd stop by my place on his way out and pick up my instrument bag? You're going to need an ID tonight anyway. May as well save some time. My back door is open, and if he'll go through the kitchen to the den, he'll find it on the shelf to the right of the door."

"What about your dog?" asked Lew.

"Mike the friendly lab? Don't worry about him."

"Did you get all that, Marlene?" asked Lew. "Good. Now patch me through to Pecore, will you please?" She waited while Marlene rang the coroner at his home. Her eye caught Osborne's: "Too much to hope for the guy to be sober, let's hope he's not too drunk to hold a camera.

"The good news," she added, "is the security firm

checks the house during the winter—said there's a key to the main entrance in the garage.

"I have no idea, Irv," said Lew, her voice testy. "Could be self-inflicted, could be homicide. How the hell would I know—I'm looking through a goddam window. Now listen to me—I need you and your camera out here *now*."

Listening, she screwed her face in anger. "Irv, what do you think you're paid for? You can tape the damn game." She took a deep breath. "Yes, please. Alert the ambulance crew we'll need transport later, but I'll call when we're ready. Got that? Thank you."

"Oh, that man," she said, hanging up. "Tried to tell me he had to finish watching a hockey game on ESPN. Of course, he's been drinking. I tell you, Doc, I want to be elected sheriff if only because four deputy medical examiners come with the county—so guess who I won't have to use."

"Yeah, but pity the poor guy who takes your place, Lew."

The position of Loon Lake coroner is an appointed one. Irv Pecore, purporting to having been schooled as a pathologist, had managed to parlay family connections to the mayor's office into thirty-some years of salaried incompetence, years during which he demonstrated a knack for mangling the chain of custody for evidence in dozens of cases.

Lazy and disorganized under previous heads of the Loon Lake Police Department, he balked at Lew's efforts to clean up the coroner's office. Her first mission had been to put a lid on his longtime habit of letting his golden retrievers wander through the autopsy room while he was working. No one else had managed to do it. True, the number of autopsies had dropped as the cost rose but, even so, bereaved relatives should not have to worry about inappropriate canine attention to their dearly departed.

That wasn't the worst of it, however. Just two months earlier, while searching for the evidence needed for a case going to trial, Lew had unearthed a cardboard box containing unidentified skeletal remains. That was on the heels of discovering that for years Pecore had stored his records in unlocked rooms and hallways where family, friends, and funeral directors, not to mention dogs, had wandered freely.

From Lew's perspective, Irv Pecore's very presence was a hazard to a successful investigation.

thirteen

She was used to take delight, with her fair hand
To angle in the Nile, where the glad fish,
As if they knew who 'twas sought to deceive them,
Contended to be taken.

—Plutarch (describing Cleopatra)

"**If** that poor soul with half their head missing is who we think it is," said Lew, as they headed back toward the long driveway, "this is going to be a long night."

"Say, look at the size of this mailbox," said Osborne, stopping and running his flashlight up and down. "Sorry to interrupt, Lew—but I've never seen a private box so big." Dark green and big enough to hold good-sized packages, the metal container was planted in cement across the road from the gated entrance to the estate.

"Guess I shouldn't be surprised. Hope Kelly has worked summers from here for years," said Osborne. "During an office visit years ago, she explained how she does it. Her staff in Madison culls letters from the thousands she gets every week—and sends them up here. She picks the ones she wants to answer in her column, writes the column, and sends it on to her editor at a newspaper syndicate. Eighty million readers, they say—pretty amazing it all comes down to just one person living on a lake in the boondocks."

"Yeah, well—could be eighty million disappointed people tomorrow. How long would you say she's been doing this?"

"Thirty-some years, maybe longer. *Time* put her on their cover for her twenty-fifth anniversary, even mentioned that Loon Lake was her favorite place to write. The Chamber of Commerce used that quote for years. Never read the column myself—but Mary Lee was a big fan of "Ask Hope." I think it's a woman's thing. Do you read her, Lew?"

"I used to. Years ago. Used to be the letters were interesting, and her responses could be quippy—perceptive, funny, and good. As if she really cared. Then something changed, the column struck me as dreary. Or maybe I changed—have enough of people's problems to deal with in this job without reading about more."

On their way out to find a phone, they were able to open the entrance gate from the back, making sure to leave it open for their return. As they crossed the road to walk back through, Lew borrowed the flashlight. She bent to examine the lock. "Doesn't appear forced." She ran the beam up, across the top, and off to the right and to the left. The estate was walled in with brick and iron.

"Now that is one expensive fence . . . hand-forged, I'll bet," said Lew, admiring the delicate design running along the top of the wrought-iron grating. "So we have an enclosed property with a locked gate. Looks pretty darn secure from this side, doesn't it."

"You can always enter off the lake," said Osborne.

"True."

They walked along in silence. He caught a glimpse of her face in the moonlight. "What are you thinking?"

"That a national magazine printed the fact that she lives here. That she writes a column dealing with strong emotions and the mistakes people make. That maybe she wrote one that upset a reader—or a reader's ex-husband or wife. This is a long and lonely road, Doc. I can't wait to see just how good the security is on this place."

They continued down the drive. Only the hooting of an owl high overhead broke the silence. "This is going to be so high profile, Doc, whether it's murder or suicide—that I don't dare have Pecore do anything except shoot the scene and sign the death certificate. The minute Todd gets here, I'll radio the crime lab in Wausau."

"National news media will be all over this, Lew."

"You better believe it—the news media, the governor, no doubt a huge funeral or memorial service. Wouldn't be surprised if the president comes—or sends his wife. I may need you for help with more than the ID, Doc. Ray, too, if he's got the time."

"Whatever you need, kiddo," said Osborne, laying a hand on her shoulder, his heart lifting. He had to be the only man in Loon Lake for whom death under suspect circumstances was a good thing. It meant an excuse to spend time around his favorite fishing partner. During such times, she had one bad habit that he loved: the more stressed she was, the more likely to sneak away for an hour or two in the trout stream.

"Something about those two kids concerns me," said Lew. "They were so scared."

"You'd think they'd never seen a police officer before," said Osborne. "I'll ask Ray. He dates their mother off and on."

"Do that. Now tell me again, Doc—the Kellys' daughter lives in Madison but owns that big log home and happens to be here in Loon Lake. So I can reach her easily. Wonder where I'll find the rest of the family? There is a husband, right?"

"Yep, Ed. They had a son, but he drowned years ago. I believe Kitsy is their only child."

"And she's about how old?"

"Mid-thirties, maybe? I can check my files and tell you exactly."

Following the directions from the security firm, Lew was able to locate the alarm control box in the garage, right next to a metal unit housing circuit breakers for the entire property. The digital readout indicated that all the zones were disarmed.

"Very high-tech system they got, Doc," said Lew, picking up a clay pot resting on a shelf with gardening tools. The key was underneath.

It took thirty minutes for Todd Doucette, the younger of Lew's two full-time deputies, to arrive. Pecore followed five minutes later. By that time, all that was needed were photos, a signature, and help from the Wausau boys.

Much as Lew hated to deal with the crime lab supervisor, an old-timer who did not believe women should serve in the military or in law enforcement, tonight she was relieved to find him still in the office.

"No question who the victim is," she said. "I have

Dr. Paul Osborne here, and he used to be her dentist. He's able to identify the body and sign off on an official dental ID.

"But this is so high profile, Gordon, we need your staff's expertise. You know the family will be demanding the FBI, the CIA, the NSA—you name it. You'll want to put some thought into who should be your spokesperson on this, Gordon. I'm sure your team will be on national news." Lew's dark brown eyes smiled at Osborne as she spoke. She was no dummy.

"Oh?" She paused for his response, then said, "Not a problem, Gordon. Fair is fair. If you can have a team here early tomorrow morning—that is the least I can do for you. How much time do I have? Okay, I'll send someone around starting tomorrow. And, Gordon— thank you very much."

Hope had not changed her hairstyle in years. Not even a violent death could do much to dent it: strikingly blonde, pouffed, and frozen with hair spray. Osborne recognized her by the back of her head even before he knelt to examine what remained of the famous face.

"No, sirree, this is no suicide," said Pecore, setting up his tripod behind Osborne. "Somebody unloaded a gun in here. No doubt about that. Look at all these casings."

"Look and don't touch, Irv," said Lew, keeping an eye on every move Pecore made. "Wausau is adamant that nothing be disturbed. You take the photos—Doc and Todd will help the EMT's move the body later. Once you finish that and the paperwork, you can leave. And, Irv, not a word to anyone. I have yet to inform the family. Agreed?"

"Oh, sure." Lew looked at Osborne. Pecore had a talent for dispersing incorrect info from the barstool, especially after being what he liked to call "over-served."

"I mean it, Irv. One word of this gets out and that's grounds for dismissal."

"Okay," said the wizened little man, holding his sleeved arm to his face. Between the flies and the odor, he wasn't the only one anxious to leave. Her hands gloved in plastic, Lew had unlocked the French doors to relieve the fetid air while Osborne did what he needed to with the corpse.

"I'll have to call one of my colleagues in town who's doing implants," he said. "Just eyeballing this, I can see she's had quite a bit of work done recently." Good dental work, too, to judge by what was left.

A brief stint in the military while he was in dental school had prepared Osborne for the gruesome effects of bullets on bone. Hope had been the target of more than one bullet, that much was certain. As certain as the rage behind those bullets. This was no suicide, no accident. Someone wanted her dead. Real dead.

The left side of the jaw had been torn away, exposing cheek muscle, bone fragments, and scattering teeth and dental implants. It wouldn't be until he examined the body in the autopsy room, using current dental records, that he would estimate Hope McDonald Kelly had thirty-thousand-dollars' worth of dental implants in her upper and lower jaws—giving her the mouth of a much younger woman.

That wasn't all that was unnaturally young. She had also had at least four facelifts, leaving scars in front and behind the hairline, behind the ears, and near the back of the head.

If the pathologist from Wausau was stunned, Osborne was not. Not after meeting Kitsy. Like mother, like daughter. Funny what constituted family tradition these days.

It was well past midnight when they walked down to Osborne's boat. Todd was to stay to be sure no trace evidence was disturbed overnight, since the Wausau crime lab refused to send anyone until the next morning. Lew agreed: if there was anything to be found outdoors, much better to search in daylight.

After considering the gazebo, which appeared to be brand new, she decided to set up a command post in the garage. "This place is remarkably clean," said Lew. "Even the garbage can is empty. Todd, you'll be comfortable here, don't you think?" The young police officer looked down at the air mattress and sleeping bag that he had made the mistake of carrying in his trunk.

"Not a problem, Chief."

"Think double overtime," said Lew. "You deserve it."

Lew insisted on going back with Osborne rather than taking Todd's cruiser. He wasn't surprised. The night sky was clear and studded with stars. The boat ride would refresh them both. And she still had to reach Kitsy McDonald Kelly with the bad news.

"What's this?" said Lew. She had walked out to the end of the dock to look out over the lake and felt something with her foot. She stooped to pick up the Sucrets tin. "Doc, can you shine that flashlight over here?"

He looked over her shoulder as she opened it. "Fishing lures. Someone who likes Jitterbugs for bass."

"See that one," said Osborne, pointing. "That's hand-painted by someone we know. That's one of Ray's."

As his boat moved slowly through the channel towards home, moonlight broke through the pines. A broken moon, a broken face, broken teeth.

"Loved by millions, target of one—yet one counts against all the rest," said Lew, interrupting his thought. "How does that happen, Doc?"

Osborne said nothing. He had his own question. "I'm curious, Lew. When you were on the phone with Wausau, it sounded like you were taking on even more work. How on earth—"

"Oh—no big deal. Someone's been passing marked bills from a bank in Antigo that was robbed last year. They found some in Minocqua and Rhinelander—and Gordon needs someone to check with Loon Lake merchants and gas stations. He's sending samples up with the guys in the morning. Easy stuff. I'll have Roger do it when he's finished emptying parking meters."

"I thought the Feds handled bank robberies."

"They did but these days they're all working homeland security. Gordon said it wouldn't be such a big deal, but the last bank robbed just happened to have three million in deposits from the casino in Lac du Flambeau.

"Funny thing is the two guys doing the robberies have been working their way through small towns around here for the last couple years. The take was always so small that no one wanted the expense of going after 'em. Not the banks, not their insurance companies, certainly not the local authorities. But this was too much. The tribe is not happy."

"Wow," said Osborne.

"Lewelleyn," he said as he neared the final set of channel markers. He could see her face in the light of the half-moon: eyes thoughtful, damp curls tumbling across her forehead. "Probably not the right time to tell you this," he said, "but you look like a moonlight serenade."

She smiled. Apparently it was the right time.

And much later, after she had had the difficult conversations with Hope's daughter and husband, and even though he hesitated before suggesting that she stay over, he decided to anyway: "I'll help you get an early start in the morning."

Once again the timing was right, even if it was ten minutes after two when she reached up to draw him in.

fourteen

*Trout thrive best in water with a high mineral content,
while this is the very sort of water that is worst for making Tennessee whiskey. This is why one never finds a
trout in a fifth of Jack Daniel's. Or vice versa.*

—Milford Stanley Poltroon (David Bascom)

Ed Kelly met them at the door. Wearing a light gray
suit and a black shirt open at the collar, he looked as ro-
bust, handsome, and affluent as he had three years
ago—the last time Osborne had seen him. The belly
might be slightly more rotund, but he was one of those
men blessed with appearing years younger than their
age.

If he was short on sleep due to the news of his wife's
death and catching an early flight north—Osborne
couldn't see it. No circles under *those* eyes. Having
spent his own early morning hours in the morgue with
Hope's corpse, Osborne couldn't help but wonder if it
was her husband's youthful appearance that had driven
her to so much cosmetic surgery.

No doubt she had loved him for his good looks and
hearty ways. But while Ed Kelly might guffaw with
gusto, Osborne knew him to be a man whose eyes

never smiled. Never smiled and were always watching. He had a way with a sidelong glance, as if checking to see if you were laughing at him. In Loon Lake no one dared laugh—the McDonald Trust controlled too much land, paid too much in taxes, and supported too many local causes—but no one took Ed Kelly seriously either. Never had.

A college basketball player who had lucked out when he got the daughter of a rich family pregnant, Ed had lucked out again when Hope parlayed a weekly column for a small newspaper owned by her father into becoming an icon of advice in America's newspapers. As her popularity soared, his position as her business manager segued into president and CEO of a successful publishing enterprise. A CEO who bragged that business was so good he could golf six days a week—inspiring one of Osborne's coffee buddies at McDonald's to comment: "Yep, Ed's a winner, all right. Thanks to being promoted to a level where he can do no harm, Mr. Important shoots in the low eighties."

Osborne and Lew followed Ed through the kitchen and into the enclosed porch that overlooked the deck and the lake. The doors leading to the dining room were shut, but the windows were open to the midday sun and a light breeze. The porch, furnished with white wicker antique furniture and a scattering of small, colorful Oriental rugs, was open and pleasant—full of summer and color and fun. Osborne knew the wicker was old and expensive because antique wicker had been one of Mary Lee's passions.

Lew caught Osborne's eye. He suspected they were thinking the same thing: who would guess that death had fouled this air less than twenty-four hours earlier? A murmur of voices from the dining room was the only indication that two of the team from the Wausau crime lab were still at work.

Ed crossed the room toward a table serving as a bar. Sunlight caught the sheen of his slicked-back hair and well-shaven cheeks. Osborne couldn't help observing he looked as sleek as a purebred black lab.

"So what can I get you folks? Soda? Paul, you need a beer?"

He turned to them, genial and inquiring, as if hosting a cocktail party. Maybe he was. On a table near an armchair, Osborne spotted a half-empty glass of amber liquid with two ice cubes. Some things never change. Ed Kelly was as he had been in all the years that Osborne had known him: flushed with the good looks of the Irish and a shot or two of Bushmills.

The man had a way of leaning forward on the balls of his feet as he spoke, giving the illusion of towering over a person even though, in Osborne's case, they were nearly the same height.

"Nothing for me, thank you," said Lew, backing away.

"Nor for me," said Osborne.

"Then please, sit," said Ed, taking the large armchair next to the bar. He plunked himself down and leaned forward, resting his forearms on his open knees. He reached for his drink, then checked his watch. "Kitsy is due in an hour. You have my full attention." He made his presence sound like a privilege.

"Oh, and by the way, Chief Ferris? I appreciate the work you and your people are doing. Any idea," he tipped his head to indicate the rest of the house, "when my home will be mine again? Other than this room?"

"I'm sure you understand—" said Lew, seating herself in a chair across from Ed as Osborne took a chair to her right.

"Of course, of course, up to a point," he cut her off with a wave. "I tried talking to your investigators, but they weren't very forthcoming. Shouldn't they know *something* by now?" The condescension in his voice and the shake of his head implied incompetence.

Osborne opened his notebook and jotted the phrase that came to mind: "whatta commode." He underlined the last word. Felt better.

"We know a few things, Mr. Kelly," said Lew, flipping to a clean page in her own notebook. She had decided months earlier, after deputizing Osborne to help her on a case, that it worked well to have him sit in when she did an interrogation. Two people see and hear things differently.

Osborne wasn't surprised to find that she preferred him to either of her two officers. Roger, the older of the two, was hopeless on anything more demanding than emptying parking meters or guarding hospitalized accident victims suspected of drug abuse. Todd was young and eager but too much of a bullet head. He would make up his mind and stop listening.

Osborne, thanks to years of experience with patients terrified to enter his office, much less sit in the dental chair, had perfected a technique for dealing with people under stress. More than once, Lew had commented that his voice and manner had a calming effect that encouraged people to open up when asked questions.

And he was tuned, as a dentist would have to be, to infinitesimal variations on a surface: a surface that might include the face and fleeting expressions of a liar.

"For instance," said Lew, her eyes firmly fixed on Ed's, "we know your wife died at the hand of another individual. Someone intent on firing *nine* bullets from a twenty-two pistol. *Nine* weren't necessary . . . that tells us something."

Ed shifted his eyes down and away.

"We know that the alarm system had not been triggered until the neighbor child tried the door."

"Yeah, that was strange. What's that kid doing around here anyway?"

"Your wife befriended Jennifer and encouraged her fishing off the dock. They waved or chatted almost every day. It was Jennifer who sensed something was wrong and tried to help. The point, Mr. Kelly, is that given the alarm system was armed, your wife must have let someone she knew into the house.

"As for the rest—I'll have an update later today. The team working trace evidence for us is from the Wausau Crime Lab—and they know their stuff. . . ." Lew waited, but Ed said nothing. Osborne knew she was prepared for Kelly to demand that more experienced law enforcement such as the FBI be brought in. This was his opportunity to do so—but he said nothing. Osborne made a mental note, one he did not write down.

"As far as talking to you or to your daughter—that's not appropriate. They report results to me and to the lab supervisor *only*."

"Ah, so you are the gatekeeper," said Ed, sloshing his glass of whiskey. "Well . . . let me rephrase my question. How long do you figure I'll need to be up here? Got an international business to run in Madison, you know."

This time Osborne did jot a note: Ed looked less bereaved than eager—as if his wife's death was a business deal that needed closing—fast.

"I can't answer that," said Lew. "But I suggest you plan to stay several days, both you and your daughter, while the investigation gets underway. I've deputized Dr. Osborne here to help out since he's familiar with your wife's family and their history in the community. I want you to feel free to call him at any time if something comes to mind.

"Now, I have a serious concern that within a few hours you, your daughter, and myself, not to mention everyone in Loon Lake, are going to be swamped with television crews, newspaper reporters—"

"No, no, no," said Ed, dismissing her concern with an airy wave. "That won't be a problem. I've taken care of all that."

"You have?" asked Lew, surprised.

It was not the first surprise of the morning.

fifteen

She is neither fish nor flesh nor good red herring.

—John Heywood

Osborne had awakened to the sound of voices in his kitchen. Lew, wearing his bathrobe, was drinking coffee with Ray. And it wasn't even six yet.

"Jeez, Ray," said Osborne as he reached to pour himself a cup of coffee, "how many times have I asked you not to drop in before—"

"Hold on, Doc," said Lew, raising one hand. "I called him. Woke up early and couldn't get back to sleep, kept thinking about this." She pointed to the Sucrets box, which was sitting open on the kitchen table.

Ray looked back and forth at the two of them, making sure it was safe to continue.

"Go on," said Lew.

"Like I said a minute ago," said Ray, "I gave Jenny half a dozen of my smaller lures—including that Jitterbug—for her birthday. The kid loves to fish smallies."

"And you gave 'em to her in this same box."

"Oh, yeah. Easy to keep in her back pocket. She was so excited to get those—I'm surprised she left it somewhere."

"Me, too," said Lew, looking at the clock on the kitchen wall. "Darn, too early to call her house. What do you think, Ray—if I wait until seven? Is that too soon?"

"Want me to call?" asked Ray. "She knows that I know she was fishing the shoreline over on Secret Lake. Might be easier for me to get her to talk."

"Do you mind? But talk to her mother first. That child looked so terrified last night. Who knows what she saw."

"Let's hope she didn't see it happen," said Ray. "What an awful thing that could be. . . . Tell you what—why don't I just drive on over there and give you a call after I chat with Jill. That's her mom. We're good friends." Lew cocked her head, eyebrows raised. "Okay, better than good friends. Jenny won't be afraid to talk to me."

"Ray, you just said something that worries me," said Lew. "If that girl did see it happen, whoever killed Hope McDonald might go after her. If that's the case, we've got to be sure that information does not get out. Her mother, the little brother—they need to know that."

"You betcha," said Ray. He threw the rest of his coffee in the sink and headed for the back door. Then he stopped. "I assume you've spoken with Kitsy?"

Lew nodded. "And her father. Meeting with each of them later today."

"How did Kitsy take it?" asked Ray.

"Well . . . I'm not sure it registered. I woke her up, of course. She was groggy, glassy-eyed. Kept trying to focus. I think she'd taken sleeping pills. Sure seemed difficult for her to grasp what I was saying. I ended up placing the call to her father with her sitting beside me. After I told him what we found and the situation, I went to put her on the phone, and she was asleep. I managed to keep her awake long enough for the two of them to talk, but they couldn't have said more than twenty words to each other."

"Was she drunk?" said Osborne.

"No. Dopey. Had to be sleeping pills or a strong tranquilizer—maybe she'd been drinking earlier, then took something."

"Ouch," said Osborne.

"Whatever—it was hopeless. I told her to go back to bed, and we'd go over details today. And I tried to make it clear she was *not* to go to her mother's home, but who knows if that registered. It was strange— I don't think I was in that house more than twenty minutes."

"Lew, something I saw yesterday that I didn't think of until just now," said Osborne. "When Kitsy was helping me get the bags with our lunch supplies, she got a call on her cell phone, opened her backpack, and a small handgun in a fancy red leather holster fell out. I'm pretty sure it was a twenty-two pistol."

Lew raised her eyebrows. "You positive?"

"No."

"What about her friend, Julia, who's staying there," Ray inquired. "Did you talk to her?"

"Kitsy insisted she was alone," said Lew.

"Really? I could swear Julia was staying there. Well, heck, this is going to be a big deal, Chief," said Ray. "Hope McDonald is like one of the most famous women in America."

"No need to tell me that," said Lew. "A couple of the

Wausau boys are meeting me at the McDonald place right at seven. I'll work with them and hope that Roger and Todd can keep everything running smoothly around town."

She glanced between Osborne and Ray. "Any chance you two can give me forty-eight hours of your time while I figure out what I'm dealing with?"

Both men nodded.

"Good. Ray, call me the minute you've talked with the girl."

It was nine A.M. when Lew and Osborne sat down at a weathered picnic table in the yard of the little house catty-corner from the gate leading down to the McDonald estate. Ray, Jill, and the two children were waiting. The morning was bright and warm and the white birches had leafed out, throwing a canopy of shade over the table.

Osborne recognized Jennifer's mother. She was a waitress at the Fireside, a dinner club where he had eaten often after fishing lakes west of town. Petite with a square, elfin face and huge brown eyes, she was wearing her hair pulled back in a short ponytail and no makeup to hide the fatigue in her face.

Jennifer was her mother in miniature: big eyes, ponytail—even the fatigue. But she did seem calmer this morning, perhaps because she was holding tight to Ray's right hand.

"Jenny did *not* see it happen," Ray had said as they walked across the road towards the little group.

"Thank goodness," said Osborne, exhaling with relief. What the child had seen was bad enough.

"So, Jenny sweetie," said Ray when everyone was

settled, "tell Chief Ferris exactly what you did last night, and why you were so worried."

The girl took a deep breath. When she had finished telling them what she had seen or not seen over the previous three days, and why she had trespassed onto the McDonald property, Lew said, "Jennifer, you have no idea how helpful this is."

"I should have told you last night," said the girl. "But I was so scared." Tears welled in her eyes.

"That's okay, it's okay," said Lew. "The important thing is that we now know it was you who set off the alarm when you tried the door handle. That's important. And the fact that you think you saw Mrs. McDonald sitting in the same spot for three nights gives me a better idea of when she may have been killed."

"Oh . . ." said Jill, "so it wasn't suicide?" She had been serious before, now she looked frightened.

"Very much not suicide," said Lew. "That's why I need to get from each of you a list of all the people you've seen coming and going through that gate. Or any unusual traffic on this road. Jennifer?"

"No one in the last couple days," said the girl.

"What about her daughter?"

"If you mean that Kitsy, the one with the tattoos? She hasn't come to visit for a long time—like a couple weeks maybe."

Lew raised her eyebrows and looked at Ray and Osborne.

"I wonder if we're talking about the same person," said Ray. "I don't remember seeing any tattoos on Kitsy—and I saw a lot of Kitsy. What sort of tattoos, Jenny?"

"The makeup stuff. Like her lips are tattooed red and her eyes—all those black lines are tattooed on."

Osborne and Ray looked puzzled. "How do you know that?" asked Osborne.

"Oh, she showed me," said Jennifer. "On Memorial Day I went over to fish, and she was on the dock in her swimming suit getting a tan. Mrs. McDonald was there, too. She was sitting in a chair reading. When she saw me, she invited me to visit with them—they got me a Coke.

"Kitsy was reading *People* magazine and showed me this article about girls getting their makeup tattooed on. She asked me what I thought—then she showed me hers—like on her eyes and stuff. She said the tattoos are a lot less expensive than buying makeup."

"I wondered why you asked me about that," said Jill, shaking her head. "Honestly. What next?"

"She used to visit her mom a lot," said Jennifer. "But not lately."

"She has her own house farther down the road, right?" asked Lew.

"Jennifer," said Jill, "tell Chief Ferris what you told me about Kitsy and her mother."

"Mom . . . do I have to?"

"Jennifer is worried that she has been doing the wrong thing fishing over there," said Jill. "And maybe she has—but she told me about something she saw and heard a couple weeks ago that I think—now that you tell me Mrs. McDonald didn't commit suicide—could be important."

"Jennifer," said Lew, "the lakes and the rivers are public property. You are allowed to fish wherever you please. On the other hand, why don't you tell me how you get over to Secret Lake?"

"The path behind their fence," said Jennifer in a small voice.

"Well, that is private land, but you've said that Mrs. McDonald was okay with your fishing over there, right?"

Jennifer nodded.

"Then you've done nothing wrong."

"So tell them, honey," said Jill. "About the fight."

"I heard Mrs. McDonald get real mad at Kitsy, and I think that's why I haven't seen her go there since. See, she used to always drive in around four o'clock every day, and she doesn't do that anymore."

"Where were you when you heard the fight?" asked Lew.

"Fishing by the dock. You can hear everything if the windows are open."

"I heard it, too," said Timmy. "They were screaming at each other."

"Any hitting?" said Lew.

"I don't know," said Jennifer. "I couldn't see anything. I just heard their voices. Mrs. McDonald kept screaming, 'Get out, get out, get out.' She was so mad. The other lady was crying, and she kept saying, 'I'm just trying to help—please let me help.' Kinda like that. Then she ran out on the deck, saw us, and ran back inside. That's how come I know it was Kitsy."

"Okay," said Lew, "that helps. Who else has been over there recently?"

"No one that I know of," said Jennifer. "But I might not see everyone who comes and goes. I have summer school in the mornings. . . ."

"Mrs. McDonald must have people who come to cut her grass and clean her house," said Lew.

"Oh, yeah," said Jennifer. "There's that Bunny woman, but she hasn't been there either."

"Bunny?"

"She's the maid," said Jenny. "She always wears a white dress. And that old man. The one who built the gazebo."

"Do you know his name?"

Jennifer shrugged.

"The garbage man," said Timmy. "That scary-lookin' guy."

"That would be Darryl Wolniewicz—good buddy of mine. May look scary, but he's a very nice man," said Ray, in a tone that reminded the kids not to judge a person on their looks.

"Okay, and the garbage man. Anyone else? What about Mr. Kelly, Mrs. McDonald's husband? Doesn't he come pretty often?"

"If he's the one who drives the big white car, he came one weekend," said Jenny. "A while ago."

"Memorial Day?" asked her mother.

"No, Mom, before that."

"You know," said Jill, "I thought it was odd that they had no party this year. They used to always have lots of visitors on the big holidays. Definitely not this year. Funny, now that I think of it."

"So what you're telling me is that Mrs. McDonald was alone most of the time," said Lew. "I'm surprised. I would have thought such a famous, prominent person would have too many people around."

"It used to be that way," said Jill. "When I moved in here four years ago, once the weather warmed, there was a constant stream—but things changed this past year. It's been very quiet."

"What about Mrs. McDonald? Did she change?" asked Osborne. He had a vivid memory of Hope's last appointment—she was vivacious, funny even. A petite, striking-looking woman, her personality always made her seem taller. She filled a room with her warmth and laughter. So much so that if her tall, handsome husband was there, you barely noticed him.

"I don't think she changed," said Jennifer. "She always waved and smiled at me. Mom, she wasn't alone *all* the time. Some days she drove to the Loon Lake Market and the drugstore."

"In the green car?" asked Lew. "The green Explorer. The car that's in the garage?"

"Yes—she would wave when she drove by."

"When was the last time you saw her drive by?" asked Lew.

"That's the thing," said Jennifer, "not for a long time—two weeks maybe?"

"So . . . around the time she had the fight with her daughter?"

"Yeah, I think so. One more thing . . . sometimes I could hear her talking. But I wouldn't hear anyone else—just her voice. Like she was talking to herself."

"And you fished there how often, Jennifer—every day?"

"She never said I couldn't." Worry filled the child's eyes.

"Not to worry, kiddo," said Lew. "You had permission."

•   •   •

"Good to know it was Jennifer who tried the door and set off the alarm," said Lew as she and Osborne walked back down the driveway to the estate.

"Better to know we don't have to worry about someone going after her," said Osborne.

"What puzzles me, Doc," said Lew, "is that as of eight thirty this morning and having checked all the doors and windows in that big house, the Wausau boys could find no sign of anyone breaking in. Whoever killed Hope McDonald had to be someone she knew, someone she had no problem letting into her home."

"Or," said Osborne, "someone who had no problem getting into her home. Not necessarily the same thing."

sixteen

There is nothing which in a moment makes a tired, despondent, perhaps hopeless man suddenly become alert and keen as the hooking of a big fish.

—Gilfrid Hartley

Ed Kelly set his drink on the table and, clasping both hands together, dropped them between his knees as he leaned forward. He cleared his throat and waited, then swiveled his flushed, square face from Lew to Osborne and back to Lew as he said, "The press is covered. My buddies at Hope's newspaper syndicate are taking care of it. They know all the top dogs and will make sure that any inquiries go to my Madison office. I briefed the staff this morning."

"Really?" asked Lew. "What are you telling people?"

"That my wife died at home of undetermined causes—and that we'll have a press release sometime in the next few days. Are you aware the Packers fired their coach last night, and the president was rushed to the hospital with chest pains? Hope's death is not likely to be high on any news budget today."

"The coroner's filing will certainly spark interest from local reporters," said Lew.

"Taken care of. Called your man Pecore at the morgue right after my plane landed this morning. Wanted to make sure he records Hope's death under her legal surname, which is Catherine Hope McDonald Kelly. I doubt the local press will make the connection."

"Well, you've got everything under control," said Lew. "Fast work."

"I've been preparing for this," said Ed with a grimace. "You see," he pursed his lips and wrinkled his brow, "this spring my wife was diagnosed with Alzheimer's—early stages but. . . ." He gave a heavy sigh. "We were told to expect a swift decline."

The room was quiet. A robin trilled. "I'm very sorry to hear that," said Lew.

Ed nodded. "Not as sorry as we were."

"Ed," Osborne asked, "if that's the case, why was she living here all alone?"

"That was about to change. We—meaning my daughter and I—were hoping to hire nursing staff to care for her. But she has been damned difficult to deal with these past weeks. There were good days when she was herself—then she'd go wacko on us. This is not a predictable disease, you know.

"Kitsy has been driving back and forth from Madison since mid-May. But she needed a break. We thought Hope would be okay on her own for just a week while Kitsy finished moving into her new house."

"*Two* weeks is how long your daughter has been in her new home," said Lew. "Maybe you can help me with something, Mr. Kelly. I've been trying to figure out why this house has bags of potato chips stashed everywhere. I went through it this morning with the team from the crime lab, and we were dumbfounded."

"Potato chips?" Ed looked surprised. "What do you mean?"

"Under the furniture, on every kitchen shelf, in clothes closets, linen closets," said Lew. "Everywhere you look there are bags of potato chips. Some opened, some not. There are potato chips in the bathrooms!"

Ed opened his mouth to protest, but Lew put up her hand—"Let me finish. Oddly enough, Mr. Kelly, your wife's office is the only room where *there are no potato chips*. And it's quite tidy—as if someone came in and straightened it up."

Ed threw his hands into the air. "I don't know. Since this all started it's been one bizarre act by Hope after another. Hell, she accused me of having another family hidden away, of stealing from her—who knows what she's been up to around here!

"Kitsy and I have been doing our level best to keep her mother's column going until we could make a formal announcement. Maybe Kitsy straightened the office."

"If she did that, why wouldn't she take a look around and do something about all the potato chips?" Lew shook her head. "This house must be overrun with mice, not to mention squirrels and chipmunks."

"She's been very busy with her new home. Hope had a housekeeper, but she fired her."

"Who was that?" asked Lew.

"Bunny DeLoye. She's working for Kitsy now."

"Back to the office for a minute," said Lew. "I found paperwork, which I turned over to the crime lab. One batch is letters that appear to be from readers of your wife's columns. Then typed pages that I think must be columns that Hope was working on. No computer, only an old Selectric typewriter. Could her computer be missing?"

"That's how Hope worked—on the typewriter. We never could persuade her to make the change to a computer or e-mail. What you found are the letters for the columns that need to be written, and the typed pages would be drafts of the columns due next week. She always turned them in to her syndicate editor six weeks ahead of time.

"I need those back. We've planned for Kitsy to keep the column going."

"Certainly, once I have a chance to look them over. Right now the crime lab is checking for fingerprints. But that was all we could find. There must be more somewhere."

"Damn right. Tens of thousands, but they're stored in Madison. Walls and walls of file cabinets full of letters. We have a six-person staff who do nothing but read the three to four thousand letters that arrive every day and discard hundreds, but they still add up. Why?"

"I'd like to know if your wife received any threats in the mail, a letter from a reader who may have been mentally or emotionally unstable. Any red flag that might help us find the killer."

"I hadn't thought of that," said Ed. "Hope's mail has always been full of letters from people in emotional distress—but not threatening to *her*. I don't recall her ever receiving anything like that."

"I'll be double-checking with her staff," said Lew. "I have a call in to Sheehan Davis, your wife's office manager."

"How do you know about Sheehan?"

"All the notes and memos in your wife's desk. Pretty easy to tell who does what. Since you seem to be out of the office quite a bit, I think it's prudent to touch base with the people handling the day-to-day operations."

Again Ed opened his mouth to say something but before he could, Lew asked, pen poised over her notebook, "Tell me again what your daughter's role has been these last few weeks?"

"All right," said Ed, unclasping and clasping his hands as if he was going over something for the umpteenth time. "Chief Ferris, my wife's business goes far beyond her daily column. We publish booklets on etiquette and other areas of behavior that require advice—not to mention four *books*. 'Ask Hope' is a multimillion-dollar enterprise—and I have had no intention of losing the business because of Hope's health. The plan has been for her to retire and hand over the column, under the same title, to our daughter. A seamless transition that can still happen—*will happen*. This is not brain surgery, you know." He took a swallow of his drink. "Anyone can write this crap."

Neither Lew nor Osborne said a word. He took another swallow. "I'm sure I strike you as a hard-nosed businessman—"

Lew snorted and said, "You strike me as a man with a low opinion of his wife's talent."

"Come on, it's girl stuff, I'm sorry. You read one, you've read 'em all."

"I disagree," said Lew, tipping her head, her eyes intent on Ed. She paced her words. "Back when I was a young wife and mother, I read 'Ask Hope' every day. I looked forward to it. You never knew what to expect, but you knew it would be interesting. Funny and warm. Always sympathetic and full of common sense.

"No, I really, really disagree, Mr. Kelly. Your wife made a difference in people's lives. I rarely found 'Ask Hope' to be . . ." Lew paused, searching for the right word, "frivolous."

Ed turned his head to look out a window, his face working. Osborne knew derision when he saw it. Ed had hated Hope. Right now he was having a hard time being civil to Lewellyn Ferris, too. A few more swallows and things could get interesting.

"Well, good of you to say so, Chief Ferris," said Ed, turning to her with a tight smile. "Can we move on?"

"Certainly," said Lew. "I have a few questions, and then I expect your daughter in about thirty minutes. I want to cover a few basics now, and we'll talk again later when I have the crime lab reports."

"Fire away."

"Let's start with where you've been for the last few weeks."

"Madison," said Ed. "And if you need people to vouch for my being there, I have my secretary putting together a list of names and phone numbers for you. *My* home is on Lake Monona and every afternoon the weather is decent, I golf with the same foursome. Evenings I play cards at my club. Home by eleven."

"Morning schedule?"

"In the office by nine thirty to check on things. Then lunch at the club and on to the golf course." He took another swallow.

"*Your* home," said Lew, looking down at her notes. "Doesn't Mrs. McDonald live there, too? During the winter months when she's not up here?"

"No. Hope and I haven't lived together for twenty-seven years. Not since the death of our son. That's not to say we haven't entertained as a couple, put forth a public image as a couple. But we haven't *been* a couple for a long, long time.

"I'm comfortable telling you this, by the way. Better you hear it from me than someone else."

Lew studied him before asking, "How would you characterize your relationship? Amiable? Contentious? I mean, why not divorce?"

Ed grinned. "You're kidding, of course. 'Ask Hope' divorce? Be serious. Look what divorce did to Ann Landers' column. We picked up two hundred newspapers after that made headlines. No, no reason to trash a thriving business just because two people don't want to share the same bed. And for the record, Chief Ferris," he shook a finger at Lew, "I know *lots* of couples who lead parallel lives."

"I would like a list of everyone who has worked on this property over the last few years," said Lew.

"Underway," said Ed. "When you talk to Sheehan, she should have that for you."

"I understand there's been a handyman working here within the last few days. Do you have his name?"

"No," said Ed. "Sheehan should have that. Every check Hope wrote went across her desk. Kitsy might know."

"The last question I have for you right now," said Lew, "is whether or not you have any idea who might have killed your wife."

"No." He sloshed his drink and took a deep breath. "I wish I did because it would save us all time—but I don't. And while I appreciate your wanting to check the letters, I doubt you'll find anything there either."

"I'll have those returned to you shortly. The crime lab is making photocopies so we can keep the originals. Since we found them here and they could be evidence, it will be best not to break the chain of custody."

"Fine. Just so Kitsy has something she can work with to complete those columns." He checked his watch. "You need me to identify the body, don't you? Shall I meet you in town?"

"Not necessary," said Lew, folding her notebook shut. "Dr. Osborne and your wife's current dentist took care of that early this morning. Given the condition of the body, I felt it would be wise to spare you and your daughter if we could. I don't mean to say you're not welcome to view the body if you wish. That's up to you. The pathologist from Wausau expects to complete his autopsy this afternoon—"

"No," said Ed, raising a hand. "Not if you've got what you need."

The sound of tires through the open window prompted the three of them to turn and look out. A white Lexus SUV had pulled into the circle drive. Following the slam of a car door, footsteps could be heard heading their way.

"Hey, pipsqueak!" said Ed, pulling himself up from the chair as Kitsy Kelly appeared in the doorway. She was dressed all in black, though Osborne wasn't sure her choice of garments was entirely appropriate: a tank top with no underwear to hinder the exposed cleavage, and snug black pants. A black sweater was flung over her shoulders and a black headband held her hair high

and away from her face. She did make one concession
to death: No jewelry aside from simple hoop earrings.

Ed walked over to her, his arms open. He gave her a
quick hug, which Kitsy, arms clenched to her sides, did
not return. Ed bent his knees to peer into her face. "Pipsqueak, your face is so red. Are you running a fever?
Allergies?"

"Try crying, Dad. Has an effect. Not that you would
know." She pushed his arms away and walked across
the room as Lew and Osborne stood up.

"Dr. Osborne," she said, extending a hand. "Sorry
we meet again under such awful circumstances." She
turned to Lew. "I'm Kitsy Kelly, Hope McDonald's
daughter."

"I know," said Lew. "We spoke last night. I stopped at
your home to give you the news. Don't you remember?"

Kitsy stared at her, "You did?" She closed her eyes.
"Oh, God, vaguely. I was so out of it. I am so sorry. I
took a painkiller and a muscle relaxant and that just
knocks me out. I'm having a reaction to my last Botox
injection, and I've got pain all down one side of my
head."

Ed refilled his drink. "If you folks are finished with
me, I think I'll take a walk down to the water. Is that allowed?"

"Yes," said Lew, "the area's been checked out.
Where can I reach you later? At your daughter's?"

"No," said Ed, "I'm staying over in Rhinelander—
at the Claridge. That Northwoods Golf Course they've
got over there is just excellent."

"God forbid he stay with family," said Kitsy, cross-
ing her arms and walking over to stare out the window.

"Hey!" Ed swung around, shaking a finger at his

daughter. "Remember what we discussed this morning? You stay on an even keel, you hear? We have work to do. Now, when you're done here, I'll see you over at your place. I want to go over the arrangements for your mother."

The sound of tires was heard again. A vintage black Cadillac pulled up next to the white Lexus.

"What the hell?" asked Ed, looking out the window. He turned to his daughter. "Who the hell told Lillie Wright to come out here?"

"I did," said Kitsy with a satisfied smile.

The ice cubes in Ed's drink clinked but not because he sloshed it: his hand was shaking.

seventeen

*Fly making gives us a new sense almost. We are con-
stantly on the lookout, and view everything with added
interest. Possibly we may turn it into a bug of some kind.*

—Theodore Gordon

Osborne knew the car. Everyone in Loon Lake knew
the car. The car and the fierce old woman who drove it,
and who was now marching through the front door,
across the kitchen floor, and toward the room where
they were all waiting.

She paused in the doorway and looked around.
"Chief Ferris, Doc," she said with a slight nod. When
her gaze landed on Ed, she said, "Very sorry to hear of
your loss, Edward." She sounded less sorry than angry.

"Thank you, Lillian, but who the hell told you—"

"I called her, Dad," said Kitsy, her chin thrust up
and out. "Right after you left my place this morning, I
called Lillie to see if she had a copy of Mother's will."

To Ed's credit, in spite of the red moving up his
neck, he remained calm.

"Now why would you do that, Kitsy?" he asked,
clearing his throat. "For heaven's sakes—what do you
think Chief Ferris must think of you? Less than twelve

hours since we learned that your mother is dead—murdered. And you're scrambling for a will? How thoughtless can you be?"

"Cut the riot act, Ed," said Lillie, her voice thundering through the room, as she moved closer, circling. "I'm here to put you on notice. No funny business. Not one item in this house or one piece of property held by the McDonald Trust is to change hands without my knowledge. I am the executor of Hope McDonald Kelly's estate. Do you hear me?"

How could he not? For a woman in her eighties, she had amazing volume. As she spoke, her full cheeks waggled and her black eyes glared from under tufts of white-gray brows.

Lillie Wright—the shape of her skull, the set of her eyes, the extraordinary thrust of her thick brows—had always reminded Osborne of the great horned owl that hunted the woods around his home. But unlike the owl who relishes its victim's brains, Lillie was famed for leaving her prey bloody and eviscerated on the courtroom floor. She was in the vanguard of women to practice trial law in Wisconsin.

She was also a longtime patient of Osborne's, dating back to when she had arrived in Loon Lake, which was soon after he had opened his own practice. Every year for the last twenty, she would announce her retirement but never quite get around to it.

"Having too much fun, Doc," she would say. "In a small town like this, a lawyer can't specialize so much as adapt to what happens to your clients. Keeps my office busy, I tell you. I got divorce cases, civil suits, probate—work up the wazoo. Next year—that's when I'll retire."

Then she would laugh a rolling, throaty, thunderous laugh. Over the years, Osborne had hired her twice. While he admired her expertise in the courtroom, he was more impressed with her wisdom and kindness in advising him. She was one of those rare lawyers who committed both mind and heart to the service of her client.

If she thought Ed was up to no good, chances were she was right. Right now, as if to avoid her stare, he was fidgeting with some papers in a long, flat leather wallet that he had pulled from the inside pocket of his suit coat. Kitsy had folded her arms across her chest and appeared more composed. Lew, notebook open, stood waiting.

"This is too much for me," said Ed, clearing his throat and slipping the leather case back into his pocket. "I am grieving for my wife. Would you excuse me, please?" He started out of the room, but Lillie blocked his way.

"*Hoold* up there, big boy. What's this I hear about you selling a parcel of Hope's land—two acres on the channel?" she said in a voice that sounded like tires on rough gravel.

"*Whaat!* No one is selling anything. I granted an easement to a conservation group," said Ed. He turned to Kitsy. "This is your doing, isn't it. You dummy. You always do it. You open that big mouth of yours before you have any idea what's what."

Kitsy glared at him. "You don't have the right to grant an easement."

"I have power of attorney," said Ed.

"That does not mean you can sell property," said

Lillie. "Not when it comes to the McDonald Trust. Hope and I went over those papers last month."

"Before or after my wife's diagnosis? Nothing she did in the last few weeks will stand up in court, Lillian."

"We'll have plenty of time to discuss that later," said Lillie, stone-faced. "Kitsy, if you want to come by my office later this afternoon, I'll have that copy of the will for you."

"It will be challenged," said Ed, trying for a second time to get past Lillie. She moved aside. At the doorway, Ed raised his glass as if to offer a toast. "Excuse me, everyone, I'm taking that walk down to the lake."

Kitsy plunked herself onto a wicker loveseat, dropped her face into her hands, and gave a deep sigh edged with a sob. Lillie leaned over to rub her shoulders. "Kitsy, shush, shush."

"I hate that man," said Kitsy wiping at her face. "I love him, and I hate him."

Lillie glanced over at Osborne and Lew. "Chief Ferris, Dr. Osborne—what are we trying to do here?"

"I need to have a short conversation with Kitsy, clarify a few details. You do know that Hope was murdered," said Lew.

"That's what Kitsy said when she called. Shot in the face."

"Yes. Many times. Unfortunately, that's as much as we know right now. No evidence of a break-in, unless the Wausau boys found something in the last hour. You are welcome to stay while Kitsy and I . . ."

"I'm afraid I have another appointment within the hour," said Lillie, checking her watch. "Kitsy, should we ask Chief Ferris to do this later?"

"No," Kitsy said, "I want to get it over with. I just needed your help with Dad. If he takes everything over—"

"He can't, and he knows that now," said Lillie. "But the man has always been difficult—a bully and an idiot. Who knows what's going on in his head."

Kitsy gave a sad giggle and said, "But he can't sell any of our land, right?"

"No, he cannot. Now we'll talk later," said Lillie. "Are you okay?" She leaned forward to look closer at Kitsy. "What's that around your eyes, child?"

"A makeup thing. I had eyeliner tattooed on—that way I don't have to put it on every day." Lillie shook her head.

"But you look so puffy, are you feeling alright?"

"Considering the circumstances, I'm okay. I just—I had some work done on my face, and it still hurts. Nothing serious."

Lillie straightened up. "Well, all right." She turned to Osborne. "I take it the good chief here has you working forensics again, thank goodness. Pecore is worthless."

"I deputized Doc to do a dental ID," said Lew. "The victim's face was in very bad shape, and I wanted to be sure we knew exactly what we had to work with—how many bullets she took."

"Good," said Lillie. "Dot every *I* and cross every *T* on this one."

"And since he's known the family over the years, I'm including him in my preliminary inquiries."

"Chief note-taker is what I am," said Osborne.

"You know, I miss you, Doc," said Lillie with a smile. "You retired! What were you thinking?"

"Lillie," said Osborne, "we don't all have your stamina."

"Don't kid me," she chortled, "you needed an excuse to go fishing every day."

Lew smiled at Lillie, then asked, "I assume you're representing Kitsy?"

Lillie reared back in surprise. "Not unless she needs me. Kitsy called me this morning because I've been the lawyer for the McDonald Trust since Hope's father was still alive. That's why I moved up here in the first place—had a client to pay the overhead, and a beautiful place to live."

She made a move to leave, then stopped. "Kitsy, call me later, would you please? And let me know if you need anything."

"Lillie," said Lew, "before you leave, I have a question. Since you've been the lawyer for the family trust all these years—I'm curious to know what you think may have happened here."

Lillie paused and cut her eyes towards Kitsy. "I've been thinking that over." She stared at Lew. That was as much as she was going to say.

"What's your schedule like this afternoon?" asked Lew. "Might be wise to sit down with you sooner rather than later."

"How about three o'clock?" asked Lillie.

Kitsy's answers to Lew's questions held no surprises. She confirmed that her mother's behavior had undergone a dramatic change over recent months. "At first, I wasn't sure what was going on, especially when she insisted upon moving up here in March. She always used to wait for warm weather."

"I understand, from your father, that your parents haven't lived together in years," said Lew.

"That's right, not that my dad has lacked for female companionship," said Kitsy.

"Current girlfriend?" asked Lew.

"I don't know who he's seeing now. He ended a ten-year relationship with a woman last fall. A woman five years younger than me." Kitsy's face was grim. "You know, we're not close. I don't discuss anything personal with him if I can help it."

"I understand," said Lew. "Think anyone on your mother's staff will know who the current friend is? And I'll want to check with the former girlfriend, too."

"Sheehan might. She knows where the money goes. . . ."

"Your father said that you will be taking over your mother's column?" asked Lew.

"Yes."

"So you will need to work together, won't you?" asked Lew.

"No more than he and my mother ever did. I'll do the writing, he'll do the selling—what little of that there is to handle. We have Sheehan and a publishing director, so he just puts in face time, if you know what I mean." She broke a slight smile. "We may be dysfunctional, but we function."

"I have as possible evidence two sets of paperwork from your mother's office that appear to be letters and columns," said Lew.

"You should have found a set of the columns that I was working on," said Kitsy. "I wrote those, then left them for Mother to look over and edit. The letters will be new material sent up from Madison."

"I'm having copies made, and everything will be returned to you shortly."

"That's fine," said Kitsy. "I won't be in the mood to work for a few days anyway."

"I'm surprised there are so few letters," said Lew. "I was expecting to find more."

"That's what the office sends us," said Kitsy. "About thirty every six weeks. We only run two or three in a column."

"What about personal mail?"

"Whatever you found in her office unless . . . sometimes she left stuff on the kitchen counter."

"Speaking of the kitchen," said Lew, "every cupboard is crammed with potato chips. This entire house is full of potato chips—shoved under the furniture, and crumbs everywhere. What has been going on here?"

"She wouldn't let anyone in for the last couple months. She fired Bunny who cleaned for her for years. She wouldn't let me touch anything. And, of course, Mother has never had to clean up after herself. I didn't know about the potato chips."

"But her office is in perfect condition—did you straighten it up?"

"No. I haven't been here for the last couple weeks. . . ." Kitsy's eyes teared and she raised both hands to her cheeks. "How great do I feel about *that* now. But, you know, she was acting so nutty—"

"When was the last time you talked to her?"

"Last Thursday. She called me that night and told me to call her the next morning at nine. No earlier, no later. So I did, and I asked her why she wanted me to call. She said she didn't know—and hung up."

"Do you know the name of the man who's been on

the property recently? An older man that the neighbors across the road saw doing some repairs around here."

"I know who you mean, but I don't know his name. Bunny will, I'm sure."

"And I'll find Bunny at your place?"

"Yes. She has her own apartment over the garage. I'll let her know you need to talk to her."

"Were you at home Sunday night?"

"Yes. Then the last two days I attended a fishing clinic with Ray Pradt. Dr. Osborne was there."

"She's got an alibi for Tuesday, all right," said Osborne.

"Anyone who can confirm your whereabouts Sunday—and Saturday?"

At the look on Kitsy's face, Lew raised her pen. "This doesn't mean that you are a suspect in your mother's death. I've had to ask your father exactly the same."

"I've a friend visiting who's been here since last Friday," said Kitsy. "We've been doing stuff together. Julia Wendt is her name. She's at my place now."

"That gun you carry in your backpack—do you have a license to carry it?"

"Yes."

"Why do you carry a weapon, Kitsy?"

"Umm, I was seeing a man a couple years ago who, when I said I wanted to break up, started stalking me. He would show up at my place late at night. He broke into my car. That's when I got the gun. I've just kept it since. I—this sounds dumb—I like the holster, it's cute."

"We'll need to check it out."

"Sure, it's in my backpack in the car. What kind of gun was used to kill my mother?"

"Not sure yet," said Lew. "Last question, Kitsy . . ." Lew's voice softened. "Do you have any idea who might have murdered your mother? It could have been an accident. . . ."

Kitsy's shoulders sagged, she looked sad and defeated. "I'm sure my dad told you he thinks I did."

"Why would he think that?"

"Because I killed my brother."

eighteen

It is just possible that nice guys don't catch the most fish.
But they find far more pleasure in those they do get.

—Roderick Haig-Brown

"**That's** what he likes to believe anyway. And I've no doubt he'll find a way to blame me for this, too," said Kitsy.

"So what you're saying is your father *accuses* you of killing your brother."

"Yes."

"But did you in fact?"

Kitsy shrugged. "It's all in how you look at it."

"When was this?" asked Lew.

"Long time ago. I was five and Brian was two and a half. My parents were having a party here at the summer house, and my little brother and I were playing down by the lake with our baby-sitter."

"That was Sandy Biermier," said Osborne. "I used to fish with Sandy's dad, so I certainly heard their version of what happened."

"That's right, our sitter's name was Sandy," said Kitsy. "I remember the day was really hot, and Brian and I were playing in the sand near the dock. We had our swimsuits on and were doing what little kids do on hot days. You know, splashing in the water, then running on the beach. The grown-ups were all up on the deck with their party.

"Except my dad came walking down to the dock with some people. They were all talking and drinking beer. Dad finished his, handed the bottle to Sandy and told her to run up and get him another one. So she left. Then he walked back up to the house with the people, leaving Brian and me in the sand. My little brother was filling a bucket full of sand and he wanted to mix some water in it, so he went out on the dock.

"I didn't pay attention—I was busy with my own sand pile. When Sandy came back after giving Dad his beer, she asked me where Brian was. I said he was on the dock, she said he wasn't. I said he was, too. We walked out to see if he'd fallen into one of the boats or something. Dad had a lot of boats in those days."

Kitsy closed her eyes. "I will never forget . . . he was floating in the water facedown. Sandy screamed for help and jumped in to pull him out, but he was unconscious. He died on the way to the hospital."

As if to shake the memory, Kitsy pulled off her headband and ran her fingers back through her hair. "All I know is from that day on, I have always felt my parents blamed me. No," she said with a bitter laugh, "I *know* they blamed me."

"How could they?" asked Lew. "You were five years old."

"If anyone should be blamed," said Osborne, "it's a grown-up telling a baby-sitter to leave two youngsters alone near water. Idiots know better than to do that."

"It doesn't change the fact that my father has never

forgiven me," said Kitsy. "When he came back from the hospital that afternoon, he screamed at me that I was the one who should have been watching Brian. Once when he was drunk, he accused me of pushing my brother off the dock on purpose."

Kitsy leaned back and glanced sideways out the window. Following her gaze, Osborne could see Ed Kelly down on the dock, drink in hand, rocking back and forth on the balls of his feet, looking out over the water.

Kitsy sighed. "Growing up with a father who hates you. Who looks at you like he wishes for all the world you weren't you—that you were the son he could take fishing, the son he could teach to play golf. You feel so helpless, you know. Like he said when Lillie walked in—'you always do it.' What he means is I always screw up, I always ruin things."

"I doubt that's true," said Lew, her voice brisk.

"Believe me, I've the therapist bills to second your opinion," said Kitsy. "But that doesn't stop his treating me the way he does. I'm just sure he'll find some way to make me feel responsible for Mother's death. Like I should have been sleeping here instead of at my place—whatever. It'll be my fault, you wait and see."

It was noon before Lew finished questioning Kitsy. After turning Kitsy's gun over to the team from the crime lab, she and Osborne headed back into Loon Lake together. He'd left his car in the lot behind the police department.

"Not much to go on, Doc," said Lew, pulling onto the road outside the gate. "Still no sign of a break-in. I have to hand it to the Wausau boys—they're doing a helluva job. That old place has more doors and porches than an Advent calendar and they've been checking and rechecking every possible point of entry: house, garage, dock area, front gate, deck, upper decks, everywhere. Whoever got into the house also had to get by the locked gate. We figure they had to have a key."

"At least you have shell casings from the murder weapon," said Osborne. "That's something."

"Yeah," said Lew without enthusiasm. "I gave Kitsy's pistol to the boys for analysis. It's a twenty-two, all right."

"That doesn't sound good."

"We'll see. Intuition tells me she's not a likely suspect." Lew snorted. "Not that my intuition hasn't failed me on occasion." She grinned at Osborne. "How many times have I been skunked trying to tease a big old brown trout out of a good hole? I'll match the hatch perfectly, drop my fly with absolute precision, know in my gut he has to take it . . . nada."

Osborne smiled. He liked her like this: intent on her work but happy.

"Tell you one thing, Doc," said Lew, interrupting his reverie, "I do not like guns of any kind in the hands of people who are chemically dependent. I may have to revoke Kitsy's license. Although . . ." she paused to glance over at him, "I'm kinda glad she had that today."

"Why? I would think the opposite."

"You don't hold on to a pistol you just used to kill someone. You throw it in the woods. You throw it in the water. You bury it in the garbage."

"Lewellyn, what if she did do it and doesn't remember . . . ?"

Lew gave him a long look. "For the record, Doc, I will be heartily surprised if the shell casings we found at the scene match Kitsy's gun."

"How soon will you know?"

Lew shrugged. "I'll ask Gordon when I talk to him later. In the meantime, I'm hoping his lab is able to rush the analysis from the autopsy—I sure could use a decent estimate of the time of death. That, and a lead from those letters I found, although I figure that's a long shot."

"I don't know, Lew. Between the letters you found here, and what they've got down in Madison, who knows? Just the fact that anyone could use the Internet to find Hope McDonald's home addresses—not to mention phone numbers—is creepy. Reminds me of the guy who shot John Lennon. People get fixated on celebrities, people like Hope."

"Which reminds me, Doc. Marlene radioed that the photocopies of the letters found here are on my desk. But I've got to take some time with Roger before I can go over those. He's picked up at least twenty of those marked bills around town. I have to figure out what we do next about that situation."

"Too bad you can't put it on hold for a few days. Your hands are full with this investigation."

"Unfortunately, the word is out, and Marlene's had calls from the tribal council. Someone over there is convinced that the fact the bills are showing up in such numbers could mean that the two guys who robbed the bank are from the area."

"The tribal council? What's their problem? Surely that cash was insured. . . ."

"The cash was insured, but not the goodwill. The

tribe owns the bank, and their insurance company is putting pressure on them to either build a new building or pay much higher premiums. Not to mention all the business they've lost since the robbery. No, Doc," said Lew, "I can understand the tribe's position. Would you put your savings in that bank right now?

"Also, finding these bills is a break for the Wausau boys. I can see why they want to act fast. They've been waiting a year for some to surface. The first bills were used at the Best Buy in Wausau, then the Wal-Mart over in Rhinelander—that was last month. Now, to have so many showing up in Loon Lake . . ."

"What I don't understand," Osborne asked, "is why a year after the robbery? Why now and not months ago?"

"Whoever the guys are, I'm sure they thought that waiting a year before using the cash would make it safe. This time of year—what with the tourists throwing money at everything—they figure merchants won't take the time to eyeball their twenty-dollar bills. You gotta remember, these are two men who made a major mistake during that robbery. No reason they can't make another. Greed helps, doncha know?"

"What mistake—besides robbing a bank in the first place?"

"Oh," said Lew, "I guess I didn't tell you this. This case goes way beyond one bank robbery and the tribe's loss. These two jabones have robbed seventeen banks over the last four years and every time, they have threatened the tellers not to put in the dye packs. Only this time, they got so excited when they saw they had the duffle with all the cash from the casino, they forgot about the dye packs.

"What's so silly is that of all the cash that was taken that day, only three thousand in twenties is marked. Now, you would think that with three million bucks *unmarked*—couldn't you just toss the three thousand? But, no, they have to make every penny count.

"And Gordon is right: the window of time for using that marked money is limited. Since he's got his boys working overtime on my case, the least I can do is sit down with Roger, give Gordon call, and see what he wants us to do next. Isn't it always this way, Doc? Especially during tourist season: everything at once."

"Would you like me to take a look through Hope's letters—see if there's anything that jumps out at us?"

"I never thought you'd offer," said Lew, her voice light. "That would make my day. But weren't you planning to get out on the water?"

"Gosh, no," said Osborne. "Supposed to hit ninety this afternoon. Too hot to fish. I'll just sit on my deck and read through those."

"If you'll do that, I'll be in touch with the office manager in Madison," said Lew. "See if they've flagged any disturbing letters on their end."

"Nice of Ed Kelly to detour the press. At least you don't have that to worry about."

"Not yet anyway," said Lew. "But that can change the minute I have an arrest. No matter how much control Mr. Important may think he has, there are a few things money can't buy. The press is one."

"Try harmony in the family," said Osborne. "What a razzbonya—dumping his guilt on a five-year-old."

"I suppose it helps explain his daughter somewhat," said Lew. "You have to wonder what motivates a woman to want to look so . . . so . . . hydroponic." Lew swung the car off the highway and onto a city street. "I found it hard not to stare—that woman exposes more skin than my daughter did when she was working as a stripper at Thunder Bay. And now she takes over advising eighty million people on how to manage their lives? 'How to make it through the night' from a woman who spends her own nights blotto on painkillers so potent she can't remember a thirty-minute conversation with a police officer informing her of her mother's death?" Lew shook her head. "Unbelievable."

"If Kitsy Kelly is capable of shooting anyone, I would hope it would be her father," said Osborne. Lew looked over at him as she pulled the police cruiser into the parking spot next to his car.

"I'm looking for a killer consumed with rage. . . ."

"Well, if it were Kitsy, don't you agree the target would have to be Ed Kelly, not her mother?"

"Can't be sure of that."

Osborne thought of his own daughter, Mallory, and the coldness between them for so many years. Years when she and her mother had shut him out. Maybe Lew had a point. Now that he and Mallory were working hard to find their way toward each other with a friendship that might even turn into love someday—he could see her questioning the things her mother had done and said. Between AA and therapy, Mallory was learning that he wasn't quite the bad guy Mary Lee had made him out to be.

"Think about it, Doc. Where was Hope McDonald the day her little boy drowned? Where was Hope when Ed said things that broke a little girl's heart?"

nineteen

When you bait your hook with your heart, the fish always bite!

—John Burroughs

It was so breezy outdoors that Osborne decided to work at the kitchen table. He set the two manila envelopes down, filled a tall glass with ice cubes and cold tap water, then sat down with a fresh pad of yellow legal paper and his favorite pen. He slipped the pages out of the first envelope and shuffled them into a neat pile. These were the draft columns, typed on 8½ by 11 sheets of paper and dotted with edits made with a blue pencil.

He opened the second envelope and slid out copies of letters sent to Hope. Stapled to each letter was a copy of the envelope in which it had been sent. Good, he thought, return addresses and postmarks. Osborne pushed back in his chair and rested his feet on the seat of the chair to his left. He decided to read through the columns first.

As he leaned back to read the first column, he heard a car slow down and pull into the driveway. A door slammed.

"Hey, Dad!" Erin's face appeared in the window over the kitchen sink. "Will you be seeing or talking to Lew this afternoon?"

"I hope so, why?"

"Would you remind her that I'm picking her up at six to canvass the homes north of Highway Forty-seven and up around Spider Lake, Black Lake—that whole area. Lots of registered voters in there, so if she can shake forty hands tonight, we'll have a shot at working the entire county before the election."

"I should be seeing her at Lillian Wright's office around three o'clock. But, Erin, she has so much going on right now—I'm not sure she can take the time."

"She doesn't have a choice, Dad. Not if she wants to win this election. You tell her I said so, and I'm the manager."

"Where are the kids?"

"Swimming lessons. I'm serious, Dad. Lew has got to do this. Say, did you hear that Hope McDonald passed away?"

"Yes, I did. And there's more to it than that."

"Serious?" asked Erin. "Can you tell me about it?"

"I don't see why not. Lew is expecting it to make the news anytime now. Come inside."

When he had finished telling Erin what he had seen and heard, he asked, "Did you ever read her column?"

"Every day. Not that there's a lot to read in the *Loon Lake Daily 'Snooze,'* as you well know, Dad. But, yeah, I've read it since I was in high school. I like 'Ask Hope.' Interesting topics, good advice, and a *great* sense of humor. Sometimes cute and funny, other times quite touching. I'd seen her in the Loon Lake Market once in awhile and had the urge to tell her how much I like the column, but that seemed so goofy I never did. Dad, it's bizarre that someone would kill Hope McDonald. She's famous for helping people, for heaven's sake."

"Lew asked me to read over these columns and letters that she found in Hope's office. See if there are any red flags, anything that might have set someone off. I was just getting started when you drove up." Osborne sat forward and laid his hands on the two stacks of papers. "Would you have the time to look at a few? Since you're familiar with her writing, you might pick up on something I'd miss."

"Sure. How many you got there?"

"About twenty columns and not sure how many letters. Here, you start with this half." Erin pulled out a chair and sat down, copies of the columns in her hands.

"Interesting. I've always wondered what stuff like this looked like before it appeared in the newspaper."

They read in silence, each setting a page facedown on the table as they finished. Osborne found nothing unusual in the ones he was reading. Every column featured one or two letters starting with "Dear Hope" and continuing for several sentences. He assumed they had been shortened from the originals and the names of the letter writers had been changed. At the bottom of each page was a note to the editor at the newspaper syndicate on which booklet or book they should suggest that readers purchase. This was always followed with a reminder to include ordering information.

The requests ranged from advice on relationships and family conflicts, to needing help in dealing with busybody neighbors, or questions on the proper etiquette for funerals and weddings. Where to sit an ex-husband's new and awful wife at a child's wedding appeared to be a hot issue. Whatever advice Hope had given in an earlier column was generating ire from more than one reader. Nevertheless, nothing to kill for.

"Check this one, Erin," said Osborne, handing over a page. "It's on violence at family gatherings. That could be something."

"Okay," said Erin, "sounds better than the ones I'm reading. These are all kind of flat." Erin placed a page facedown and started the next. "Oh . . . Dad, you better look at this."

Osborne leaned over. Erin held two pages out so he could see. "On all the other columns I've read, the edits are lightly written—see? A word crossed out here, one added there."

"Yes, mine are the same," said Osborne. "Very light script, even a flourish at the end with Hope's initials."

"Okay . . . now, get a load of this." Erin slid the second page across the table.

Blue pencil scrawled across the typed letters and responses. The blue markings were so heavy he could imagine the pencil lead breaking off.

"Read the edits." She pointed with a finger.

After reading just two of the scrawled comments, Osborne could hear rather than see the anger behind the rantings. Obscenities sprawled across the typed lines, and one sentence was etched across the top: "This is utter stupidity! You're fired! I don't want you near this house again. You slut . . ." The last word ran off the page.

"Is this a joke?" asked Erin. "Look, Dad." She laid the page on the table and set two of the others beside it. "Whoever did the other edits wrote this, too. It's the same handwriting. Who is it, do you think—the daughter?"

"According to the note attached to the first column in the set," said Osborne, "Kitsy wrote the columns and is asking her mother to check for any corrections or changes she would like to make. We have to assume the blue pencil markings are Hope's."

"I wonder what set her off?" asked Erin, scanning the page again. "The letters and answers are typical of the other columns. But, man, she goes berserk on this page. I wouldn't want to be the person getting hammered like this.

"Let's check those letters, Dad," said Erin, pointing to the second stack of copies.

"I'll take half, you take half," said Osborne.

"Oh, I see," said Erin after rifling through the top pages, "these are letters that haven't been answered yet."

"Right," said Osborne. "These were also found on Hope's desk, still in their original envelopes. Another set of copies will go to Kitsy. Just like she did with the columns we just read, she'll write these up into new 'Ask Hope' columns."

"Gotcha," said Erin, studying each letter. Some ran on for pages, most were handwritten, and each one had a photocopy of its envelope stapled to it.

Osborne was midway through his half when he came to a photocopy of a card. The note was brief and handwritten in a loopy scrawl. "Check this out," he said, handing it to Erin.

"Poor penmanship," she said, then read it out loud:

"Dearest Hope,
     How can I begin to thank you? The land you've given me is more than just land—it's a reason to live.

I love you dearly and thank you, thank you, thank you.

 D."

"Guess what," said Osborne, waving the photocopy of the envelope that had contained the card. "This has no postmark, no address, only 'For Hope' written across the front. It was never mailed. Someone either dropped it into her mailbox or left it in her home."

"Or handed it to her. Do you think it's from a lover?"

"Could be," said Osborne as he called Lew's direct number.

Marlene picked up. "She's in a meeting, Doc. Is this something I should break in for?"

Osborne looked over at Erin. "I think you better."

twenty

Bait, n. A preparation that renders the hook more palatable. The best kind is beauty.

—Ambrose Bierce

Lew was in a meeting with Roger when Osborne got to her office. The door was open and as he poked his head through, she waved him in. "Hey, Doc, maybe you can help us out here."

"Right now? It's almost three, Lew. Shouldn't we heading over to Lillie Wright's?" Osborne hesitated in the doorway.

"Not to worry. She called and moved us back to three thirty—a client dropped in unexpectedly. Come on in, take that chair next to Roger, and let me show you these photos."

With a nod to the patrol officer, Osborne sat down. He loved this room in the old courthouse with its high ceilings and sash-hung windows open to the sun and fresh air. Asparagus ferns, just like the ones he'd had in his waiting room, cascaded spring green and feathery over the windowsills.

From across her neatly organized desk, Lew watched him, waiting until he was settled, her dark eyes excited. "You won't believe the quality of these images," she said, handing him an eight-by-ten photograph. "Just excellent."

The photo was grainy but surprisingly well-detailed. "Wausau sent them up this morning. That last bank that was robbed got this photo with their surveillance camera. Pretty good huh? We're lucky—it was a new bank building with state-of-the-art equipment."

The closer he looked, the more Osborne was surprised at how much detail came through. The two men stood shoulder to shoulder at the teller's window, close enough for the camera to frame both from the chest up. They were dressed in light-colored long-sleeved shirts, loose overalls, and wearing black masks that covered their heads but left their eyes exposed. Their eyes and an oblong expanse of skin and bone. Each mask fit so tight to the head, it was easy to see the line of the jaw, the width between the temples.

"I'll bet those are nylon snowmobile masks they're wearing," said Osborne, referring to the headgear worn under helmets. Snowmobile helmets have to fit tight to the head, as do the face masks designed to prevent frostbite at high speeds. As he studied the print he was struck by how well the two heads were silhouetted against the light shirts, the exposed necks, and the well-lit background.

"I can't get over it," said Lew. "The detail is so good, I can make out just about everything on that desk behind them, and that has to be a good ten feet away."

"I can see the bands on the bills the teller is handing 'em," said Roger. "Chief, what I don't understand is why that teller didn't hit the alarm button. Don't they all have one?"

"Whether they do or not isn't a factor," said Lew. "Isn't a factor if it's a country bank like this or one in New York City. Tellers today are directed to treat a holdup like any other withdrawal—just hand over the cash and don't make waves. Do nothing to upset anyone, especially the perp."

"Really," said Osborne. "I didn't know that."

"You want to know why bank robberies are up a hundred sixty-seven percent this past year? Cheaper to collect from an insurance company than to be sued over the death of an employee. Most bank jobs net under ten thousand bucks. These jabones got lucky; they hit the tribe's bank just as the casino deposits had arrived. Man, if we could see their mouths through all that nylon, you know we'd see big smiles."

"Yep," said Roger, nodding his bald head, "really big smiles."

"Roger's going to show this around to every gas station and shop where the marked bills have been passed," said Lew, "but before he does that, I wanted to see if we could flag some distinguishing characteristics that might jog a memory.

"For instance," she added as she picked up her own copy of the photo and pointed at it with a pen, "I see two people, one heavy, one thin."

"Not heavy so much as stocky," said Osborne, looking at the photo closely. "I'd use the word *stocky*, Lew."

Since the two figures were standing side by side and wearing loose clothing, it wasn't all that easy to see the difference in physical builds. "I'd say the one on the right is a good three inches taller than the other. . . ."

"Y'know, Chief," said Roger, "if they measure the

height of the teller's cage and we compare, then we'll know exactly how tall these two are."

"Good thinking, Roger, and Wausau did exactly that. The one on the right is five-foot-eight, the other five-six-and-a-half. Short guys."

"Darn, I wish we could see their hair." Roger shook his head in frustration.

"Well, that's no help," said Lew. "These two were so innocuous looking that all any witnesses could recall was that they both had mullets."

"What's a mullet?" asked Osborne.

"Oh, one of those haircuts you see around here on men *and* women," said Lew. "Chopped short in the front and on the sides, longish in the back. Popular with the heavy-metal crowd. I think they were wearing wigs."

"Well . . . I'll tell you two something," said Osborne, sitting back and allowing himself to feel superior for a brief moment, "I can see something better than hair. The bone structure of the upper quadrant of the head—all this area around the eyes," he said, pointing. "Any chance we can blow this up, Lew? I would really like to see those heads up close."

"I thought you'd never ask," said Lew with a grin. "I wasn't holding back on you, I just wanted your first impression on seeing our Bobbsey Twins here side by side. The lab did this for us. . . ."

She handed Roger and Osborne each three enlargements. The first showed both heads, the first frame blown up. The second and third were blowups of each head alone.

"Whoa," said Osborne, sitting straighter in his chair. "This close-up of the two heads in one frame . . . the lighting is so good and the masks fit so well that I can see the shape of the skulls. Lew," Osborne added as he shifted his chair so she could see his photo, "this bone structure above the eyes and the cheekbones . . . these aren't men. You're looking at two women."

"No," said Lew. "Two *women*?"

"Now, how the hell—" said Roger, pulling his chair closer to the edge of the desk so he could better lean over the photo in front of him. "The people in the bank would know they were women, don't ya think?"

"Way people dress today?" asked Lew. "I don't think so. Not to mention that old saw: 'The worst witness is an eyewitness.' "

"The tightness of those masks emphasizes the shape of the skulls," said Osborne. "The area above the eyes exposes the structure of the brows, the area below the cheekbones.

"Now, as a dentist who spent forty years working inside heads, let me assure you of a few facts. One, the male skull has a square jaw and a heavy brow, along with bumps and knots where muscles are anchored. Two, the female skull is markedly smoother with beveled edges. We were taught, in anatomy class, to call the female skull and skeleton *gracilis*—because it is graceful, lovelier than a man's.

"Thanks to the lighting and the light clothing these two are wearing, not to mention their bare necks, I can see the curve of the jaw on each one." Osborne leaned forward in his chair. "Lew, I'm ninety percent sure these heads are *gracilis*."

"I don't see it," said Roger, shaking his head in disbelief.

"Think Pecore would pick up on this?" asked Lew.

"He might," said Osborne. "Any pathologist can tell you if a skeleton is male or female from the bones. Skulls are the best identifiers—I know a female when I see one."

"I dunno," said Roger, "I think those two just walking in there, people'd know it was two women. And what about their voices? That's a dead giveaway."

"They never said a word. That was their M.O.," said Lew. "They picked a teller who was relatively isolated, handed her a note, and showed her a handgun. No more questions. And they pulled this dozens of times over the last three years.

"So what do you think, Roger—does that help?" Lew stood to signal their meeting was over.

"Yep," said Roger, pushing himself up from his chair. He didn't seem entirely convinced. "So now you want me to show people these photos and tell 'em it's two gals been pushing the pink bills, right?"

"That's the story, and the sooner the better."

"Pink bills?" asked Osborne.

"Here." Lew handed him a twenty. At first glance it looked legitimate but once he examined it more closely, he could see it was indeed tinged pale pink. "Easy to miss on a busy day in the Loon Lake Market," she said, "especially with teenagers at the cash registers."

"Why are they so lightly colored?" Osborne turned the bill over in his hands. He would never have spotted it.

"The dye pack exploded red," said Lew, "but our industrious duo countered that with a good laundering. Who knows how many times they put the money through the washing machine. Hence we got pink.

"Roger," said Lew, opening the door to usher him out, "please, do your best to get to every place where the bills were passed as soon as possible."

"You want me working overtime?" His eyes flickered with hope.

"If that means I can get you on the street with these tonight, by all means." Osborne half-expected to hear him skipping down the hall.

"May I hold on to these photos, Lew?" he asked as Lew returned to her desk and sat down. "I'd like to study these some more. This shot of the thinner one . . . something about the line of that lower jaw . . ."

"Doc, whatever you want. I am going to look so good in Wausau—those guys . . . whoa, will they be peeved. Now show me this letter you found."

"Not just a letter, Lew, we found a column marked up differently from all the others. . . ." He set the page on the desk in front of Lew with one beside it for comparison. "And there's this letter." He handed it over, then sat back to watch her face as she studied first the marked-up column, then the letter.

"Kitsy wrote the columns on her mother's behalf, is that right?"

"Yes."

"So she appeared to be taking quite a beating, wouldn't you say?"

"Yes, indeed. Spoken or written, words hurt."

"And this letter—I have got to meet with that housekeeper as soon as possible. If anyone knows who was coming and going, who might have dropped this off—it has to be her. I'm driving out to Kitsy's to question her right after we see Lillie."

"You haven't forgotten Erin is picking you up at six to canvass an area this evening, Lew."

"Oh, damn. I can't do that tonight. Well, maybe. I'll see how the meeting goes with Lillie—if it's short. . . .

As they walked down the hall toward the parking lot, Lew said, "Jeez Louise. What a day—I'm working way too hard. No time to fish, no time to fool around. . . ." She poked him with her elbow. "Do I really want to be sheriff and have so much more to handle?"

"Eh, you'll have a larger staff, Lew. That will make a difference. This is unusual, you never have this much going on. And not only do I think you would love that job. I know people who want you to have it."

The moment he said it, he knew she was right. If Lew Ferris were elected sheriff, they would have very little time together. Good-bye fishing, good-bye. . . .

twenty-one

The great fish eat the small.

—Alexander Barclay

Lillie Wright's office was in her home, a small bungalow four blocks from the courthouse and one of the few stucco houses in Loon Lake. The mottled green-and-cream stucco was covered with ivy, which also hung heavy over the wide stairs leading up to the front door.

Lew and Osborne let themselves through the gate in the picket fence surrounding the house. "Very Oriental, isn't it?" asked Lew, admiring the grasses and shrubs lining both sides of the sidewalk leading up to the house.

"Japanese. When she was younger, Lillie would travel to Japan every fall," said Osborne. "She's been working on this garden for years and told me she has planted every inch herself." They walked up the steps and onto the porch. They paused, able to see through the screen door into the front hall. Voices could be heard from inside. One a soft murmur, the other strident. No question which was Lillie's.

"You cannot go back there," she said. "You're putting your life in danger, girl."

"Oh, no, it's not that bad. I'm sure it's not." Osborne knew he'd heard that voice before, but he couldn't place it.

"Okay, then tell me this—what are you paying me for?" asked Lillie. Lew rang the doorbell.

"Chief Ferris?" Lillie called from inside.

"Yes, with Dr. Osborne. Here for our three-thirty. Want us to wait outside?"

"No, come in here. I have someone who needs help."

Osborne opened the door for Lew, and they stepped into the foyer. A door to the right was open, and Lillie sat on a futon sofa at the far end of the room. She motioned them in. Sitting in a wooden chair to her right was a face familiar to Osborne: Molly O'Brien.

"Chief Ferris, I want you to meet my client Molly McBride."

"O'Brien," said Molly standing up to shake Lew's hand. "I'm married, so it's O'Brien."

"Not for long, if I can help it," said Lillie, not moving from where she was sitting.

"McBride," said Lew. "The same as—"

"Yes," said Lillie, "the family that was murdered twenty-seven years ago. Molly was the only survivor."

"I don't remember it at all," said Molly. Osborne could see she'd been crying.

"Of course you don't—you were only two and a half years old," said Lillie. "Sit down, you two, please. Molly's run into a problem that is more serious than she knows."

"How's that?" asked Lew.

"Umm," said Molly, taking a deep breath. "Well, I'm married to Jerry O'Brien and . . . umm . . . earlier today I opened a door in his house where I'm living.

It's a door to a room that he keeps locked. Whenever he goes somewhere, I try the knob to see if it's open, but it's locked. Until this morning. I guess he forgot to lock it. And when I went inside, I found another bedroom. And in the closet and the drawers, I found women's clothing."

"That's strange," said Osborne. "You think maybe he has a girlfriend, or all that belonged to someone else he was seeing before you? Molly, you haven't been married very long, right?"

"Just about a month. The clothing . . . well, it's all like . . . a very large size."

"It belongs to Jerry," said Lillie. "No question."

"So you're thinking your new husband has some psychological problems," said Lew. "That's a matter for a mental-health professional, Molly. Cross-dressing is not a crime."

"Murder is," said Lillie.

Osborne and Lew stared at her.

"Jerry O'Brien murdered Molly's parents and her brother and the family dog twenty-seven years ago. Molly was almost three years old, just a toddler, and the only one left alive. That little child was in the house for two days with the victims."

"I know that case," said Lew. "But I thought the killer was a teenager off the reservation. Wasn't there proof that he did it?"

"The boy was my client. I felt the so-called evidence had been planted, his so-called confession was beaten out of him, and I knew that boy would never get out of jail. I was right. Within ten days of his arrest, he committed suicide. Or so they said—I doubt that, too."

"This goes back awhile, Lillie. Who was the chief of police at the time?" said Lew.

"Bob Wenzel. Mean as they come and always had it in for the Native American kids, pinned every assault-and-battery case he had on the boy. Cleaned off his desk. By the way," said Lillie to Osborne and Lew, "Molly knew none of this until half an hour ago."

"I—I don't know what to say," said Lew.

"Lillie's right about Wenzel," said Osborne. "The man was evil. But, Jeez Louise, Lillian, Jerry O'Brien has been publisher of the *Loon Lake Daily News* for years. If I remember right, he was Pat McBride's boss."

"Yes, he was. And he found the bodies. How convenient."

"I just can't believe you're right," said Molly. "He was so nice until . . ."

"Could we start at the beginning?" asked Lew. "I'm lost. How did Molly even end up here today?"

"I—"

"She—"

Molly and Lillie started talking at the same time.

"Let me go first, Molly," said Lillie. "I think I know more of the history than you do. Is that okay?" Molly nodded. "After the tragedy, Molly was sent to live with her mother's sister. That family asked me to handle the estate, and we tried to sell the family home. But, given the circumstances, that was futile. Too many rumors that it was haunted and so forth.

"Molly's aunt and I decided to close it up and keep the house and land in trust for her to inherit on her thirtieth birthday. It's a nice little house on Lake Yellow Dog—worth a lot more today than it was then."

"So I came up here a couple months ago to see it and that's when I met Jerry—"

"Which she never told me, or this wouldn't be happening," said Lillie. The fierceness in the old woman's face was terrifying even to Osborne. "I still don't understand how you could possibly end up in bed with that man."

"That's the thing," said Molly. "I never have. He told me at first that he was recovering from prostate surgery—"

"Wait, wait, wait," said Lillie. "Let me rephrase my question. What possessed a lovely young woman like yourself to even entertain being with a man like Jerry O'Brien? The sight of him makes my skin crawl."

"Now, hold on, Lillie," said Lew. "That's not fair. You have an emotional reaction to the man. In reality, he's not a bad-looking fellow."

"Here's the deal," said Molly. "I was working in television in Chicago as a news producer, a very stressful job. I was depressed, I put on weight. And I was engaged to be married to a wonderful guy. We were living together. Then he dumped me. All this right before my birthday.

"I came up here heartbroken. Mr. O'Brien—Jerry—was sweet. You know, he took me out to dinner, loved listening to me talk. We talked about the news business a lot. Before we got married, he promised to buy the station over in Rhinelander and make me news director. He just seemed so . . . so . . . comfortable. And me, I was stupid, I thought why not?—when he asked me to marry him. It felt so good to be loved, even though we barely touched.

"Sounds strange, I know. I didn't say anything to

anyone—not even my aunt, because it just seemed so nice. I didn't want any criticism that he was older than me or anything like that. So we got married a month after we met.

"And that's when things changed. The minute I had the ring on my finger, he became a different person."

"In what way?" asked Lew.

"He stopped talking to me. At first, I thought he was having a hard time adjusting to me being in his house. But then he got strange. He would go out almost every night and not tell me where he was going. I would catch him just staring at me with this angry look. Then last night, I went down in the basement to get something out of one of my boxes. He turned the light out at the top of the stairs, so I was in total darkness.

"He said things to me in the dark that were scary. Told me I was a bitch like my mother, that I was fat and ugly just like her—weird stuff. He kept me locked down there for over an hour. When he finally let me out, he laughed in this hideous way. I was so scared, I locked myself in my bedroom for the rest of the night. Then I called Lillie this morning."

"You can see why she cannot go back to that house," said Lillie. "She stays here with me until her house is ready."

"Oh," said Osborne, "you mean you're not selling that property?"

"I don't want to," said Molly. "I love it here in Loon Lake. Ever since Jerry got so weird, I've been thinking I could get a divorce and live there. So I've got people clearing the yard, which is terribly overgrown, and I'm going to have the interior painted, the floors done. . . ." Then Molly smiled for the first time, the smile that had enchanted Ray, and said, "I hope the house is haunted. I would love those ghosts."

"Lillie, I'm not sure what you want me to do," said Lew. "Reopen the case? You've got to give me a better reason than your feelings about Jerry O'Brien, you know."

"May I review the files and think this over?" asked Lillie.

"I would like to see the files," said Molly. "I would like to know more about what happened to my parents and my brother."

"Pecore lost or destroyed any evidence we might have had—that's a given," said Lillie. "That man is a miserable excuse for a coroner."

"Couldn't agree with you more," said Lew. "But while he's disorganized as hell, he never throws anything out. I wouldn't be surprised if there's not something somewhere. Let me poke around in his back room."

Molly stood up and walked towards the door. "Where are you going now?" asked Lillie.

"Back to get my stuff."

"Not without me you're not. You're not going there alone."

"I'll be fine."

"Tell you what," said Lew, getting to her feet. "I have a couple cell phones in the front office that the state has us testing. Why don't I let you use one, Molly. That way you can call if you have any problems."

"I have my own cell phone."

"The ones we have are different. Hold on, and I'll show you what I mean," said Lew as she left the room. She was back in less than a minute with a small box that she handed to Molly. "Be sure to read the manual carefully," she said. "This cell phone has a GPS locator on it—we can monitor where you are at any time using some new software in our computers. Also, it has a walkie-talkie feature, so all you need to do is press a button, and you'll reach me directly."

"Cool," said Molly. "That make you feel better, Lillie?"

The old lawyer nodded. She watched as Molly left the room with Lew.

"You think I'm a crazy old woman, don't you?" asked Lillie with a humorless cackle.

"I've known you too long not to trust your instincts," said Osborne. "It's a good thing, you're getting Molly in here with you."

"And an emergency divorce. I'll have her out of that man's grip in thirty days."

twenty-two

A rising fish. Sunset and scenery are at once forgotten.
We must get that beggar!

—George Aston

"**Hope** was *branded* by her childhood," said Lillie, her words running like tires on a gravel road. Shifting her weight on the sofa, she crossed her legs and reached one arm across the back. She was ready to talk. One thing Osborne knew from her office visits: Lillie loved to talk.

Sitting across from her, he could not imagine what she had looked like in her youth, though he knew there had been an ex-husband some fifty years ago. Hard to believe. Lillie Wright was not the least bit feminine. Not in her appearance, certainly not her voice, which boomed and bellowed as if trained for the pulpit.

She was wearing a boxy, green plaid, flannel shirt, worn khakis, and beat-up moccasins. Her thick gray hair was cropped close to her head. Old and rugged, yes—but vibrant. She moved with grace, she held your eyes as she spoke. He couldn't help but wonder if Lew, who had that same tough charisma, would look this good in her old age. Be nice if he were around to see.

While he knew Lillie to be friendly, even warm, she always had an edge. Osborne suspected she could maneuver a boat trailer, rototill a garden, and shoot a .357 Magnum as easily as any man—even in her eighties. Right now she was relaxed but all business as she answered Lew's questions about her client.

"Hope was *cursed*," said Lillie, the light in her eyes fierce. "Cursed because she was the only child of two very wealthy and self-centered people who taught her to believe you could buy *everything*. Including a child.

"They treated that little girl as if *she* had been purchased—always leaving her in the care of a nanny, a governess, a housekeeper—then boarding school, summer camp, or summer at the estate with the governess. Too busy with their travels and their social life to be bothered. When they were around, and *if* Hope was with them—it was as if she were part of the décor. Always beautifully dressed, never a hair out of place.

"But the saddest little eyes. I used to feel so sorry for her, I would take her to the old root beer stand. . . . Remember that place, Doc? Buy her a frosty root beer float . . . oh, she loved that!"

Lillie pointed a finger at Lew. "Now *you*, Chief Ferris. I see you laugh, I see you get upset with some of those razzbonyas you got working for you. I was watching you just last week over at Ralph's Sporting Goods picking out a new fly rod. The look on your face," she laughed her throaty laugh, "I had the urge to invite myself along.

"But Hope—you never knew *what* she had on her mind. In all the years I'd known that woman, seldom was she spontaneous. Always calculating, never letting her guard down. Her face was perfect all right—a perfect mask. At least in public."

"Are you saying that before the diagnosis of Alzheimer's, she was having problems?" asked Lew.

"Oh, yes. In spite of her money and her fame, Hope did not have an easy life. She disparaged her talent, for one thing. More than once she told me she felt that her father had bought her success: he owned the newspapers, and he made them run her column. What she refused to hear was that while that may have been true in the beginning, you don't last as long as she did in so many papers worldwide if you aren't damned good.

"On the other hand, she used her money to buy friends, to buy that idiot husband, to buy a beautiful lifestyle. But," said Lillie, shaking her cheeks as she spoke, "there was one thing she could not buy . . . she could not escape tragedy."

"Her parents died when their private plane went down in Lake Superior," said Osborne.

"Yes. Hope was in her mid-thirties when that happened. She was devastated. Two months later she lost that dear sweet little boy. She never got over a terrible sense of guilt about that awful, awful day."

"Kitsy told us her parents blamed her for her brother's death," said Lew.

"Really?" asked Lillie. "Hope never said any such thing to me. So far as I could see, she blamed herself. After Brian's death, she changed. She had bouts of manic depression and started drinking, taking pills. She was deeply unhappy in her marriage, and I urged her to divorce Ed. But she refused. She let him talk her into the whole public image thing—I'm sure she could have worked her way around that.

"Over the years I watched her turn into a public Hope and a private Hope. And on a bad day, let me tell you, the private Hope could be a hard woman to be around."

"That surprises me," said Lew. "I only knew her through the columns. But she seemed so wise, so understanding. Her sense of humor was priceless—"

"I never said Hope wasn't brilliant and witty, she was. But, like I said, she never gave herself enough credit. In a way, that was the secret to her success. Readers loved her because she could empathize, because she understood pain.

"But where she was an expert on telling others how to care for the people they love, she was not capable of that herself. I will bet you she never once said, 'I love you,' to that daughter of hers. What she could do in public, she couldn't do within her own family. She was an emotional cripple.

"I'm telling you this because I don't know who killed her. But this may lead you somewhere. Hope had great difficulty loving herself. Did she deliberately put herself in danger? She has before, you know."

"If you mean the plastic surgery," said Osborne, "I was astounded. She must have had at least four facelifts."

"That was Hope's way of hiding," said Lillie. "Destroy the evidence. Tears, booze, pills, inappropriate men. Those take a toll on your face, not to mention your soul. But Hope threw money at it. She paid a surgeon to cut away the consequences."

Placing both feet on the floor, Lillie leaned forward, resting her elbows on her knees. "So, okay, we've established the fact that my client was not a virtuous woman—but she was human. She tried to love, she knew hate, and she made terrible mistakes." A sad smile crossed Lillie's face. "On the other hand, how else could she have been so perceptive?"

Lew tapped her pen on her notepad, then asked, "What do you mean by 'inappropriate men'?"

"During her forties and fifties, Hope went through a string of good-looking, worthless types. But that was twenty years ago. If I thought we had a suspect in the crowd, I'd have told you this morning."

"Gigolos?"

"Along that line, yes."

"Lillie," Lew asked, "when was the last time you saw Hope?"

"Six weeks ago. She knew she was slipping, but she had lucid periods, enough for us to review her legal affairs—her will, the McDonald Trust, some bequests she wanted to make. Ed's out of his league, by the way. That threat he made this morning is ridiculous. I had Hope's physician fly up from Madison to witness her behavior. He sat in as she made her decisions. There'll be no contesting the will no matter what Ed says."

"Did she give any indication of being afraid of anything?" asked Lew. "Any person?"

"No. But one thing I did find unusual: she was adamant on wanting to be alone. 'I want solitude, Lillie,' she would say over and over. Now, much as she was comfortable in that big place of hers, she had always had help maintaining it. So it was strange that she wanted no one there. She kicked her daughter out, she fired her longtime housekeeper. She turned into a hermit. It wasn't safe, and I tried to talk her out of it."

"Chief," Osborne asked, "do you mind if I ask Lillie a question?"

"Go right ahead."

"Are you saying it wasn't safe because of her mental state?"

"Yes. And because I was expecting that she might find herself on the dock some night, down at the end where the water is deep, and accidentally fall in. Possibly with some help. That's what I have been worried about."

"Ed?" asked Lew.

Lillie shrugged. "I don't think I have to tell you two how many accidental drownings around here should have been more closely looked into—do I?"

"That may be how it used to be," said Lew. "Not while I'm head of the department."

"So call me crazy, but that's what I expected to hear from Kitsy when she called. That or suicide."

"Suicide," said Lew. "Nine bullets in the head is not suicide."

"Not unless you act in a way to precipitate that."

"Are you saying Hope might have deliberately—"

"You asked me when I saw her last. That was six weeks ago. I *spoke* with her on the phone Sunday morning. She told me she was planning a party. She called it a 'black velvet oblivion.'"

"So she was really losing it," said Lew.

"Maybe, maybe not. When it came to difficult things in life, Hope was a genius at finding someone she could pay to do it for her. In fairness, I'll admit her mental state was deteriorating, but who knows?

"After we talked, I tried to reach Kitsy. All I got was voice mail so I left a message. Then I called her former housekeeper—you know Bunny DeLoye? She wasn't home either, but I did leave a message."

"Did you call Ed?"

"God, no. She needed help, not torture. Now, of course, I blame myself for not driving out there, not following up the next day. . . ."

"But, Lillie, you're not her family," said Osborne.

"I know. Plus she had taken to accusing me of interfering. As the disease was progressing, I could see that the slightest stress caused her to become agitated. I just—I didn't want to push her too far."

"We know that Ed was in Madison—"

"Of course he was," said Lillie, interrupting Lew. "Just because I think he's an idiot doesn't mean he's not cagey."

"I get the point," said Lew. "Lillie, would you take a look at these and tell me what you think?" She handed over copies of the letter and the blue-penciled column.

Lillie examined the column first. She looked up with a sigh. "How would you feel if you were Kitsy? She did the work, you know. The idea was to keep Hope feeling involved. This is so sad. To have these be your mother's last words? Poor woman."

Osborne wasn't sure if she meant Hope or Kitsy.

"Well, this is a thank-you from Darryl Wolniewicz," said Lillie on reading the copy of the card. "Hope made him a gift of some land. The property isn't anything that Kitsy should get upset over. It's along the channel, quite a bit of wetland."

"You don't mean Carla Wolniewicz's father?" asked Osborne.

"Yes, he's the one person Hope would allow onto the property."

"How on earth did that happen?" asked Osborne.

"Whatever her state of mind, Hope still had one endearing quality," said Lillie. "She looked out for the underdog.

"You may not know this, but she did something very special over the years. When she had letters from people who were obviously suicidal, she would call the newspaper where they lived and insist that the publisher get help to that person.

"Darryl, to her, was one of those people. Early this spring she hired him to cut down some trees, and when he charged all of twenty dollars for each tree—she couldn't believe it. The lawn people wanted at least two hundred a tree! Next, she asked Darryl to clear an area where she planned to build a gazebo. About that time she asked me what I knew about him.

"Now, I've represented Darryl pro bono over the years. You know, Chief, those DWI's of his. So I told her he was harmless and had gotten kind of a rotten deal, what with that wife of his. I encouraged her hiring him. As far as I could see, it was doing them both good.

"He was like her puppy dog. He fixed the door stoop, cleaned the garage, picked up groceries. He did everything she asked—and charged so very little for his services. When she found out he loved fishing that channel, she decided to gift him some acreage."

"Do you think he had a key to the front gate?" asked Lew.

"I doubt it. Why?"

"Just curious. Where will I find Darryl?" asked Lew. "Do you have his address?"

"Only a P.O. number."

"Ray will know, Lew," said Osborne. "Darryl used to help Ray out at the cemetery."

"Lillie, is there anything else that you can think of that might help me right now?" asked Lew.

"Not at the moment. But I do need your help with Molly McBride. I'm very, very worried about that young woman."

"Right," said Lew, standing up and checking her watch. "I'll pull the files on the case tonight."

"Do more than that," said Lillie. "See if any of the evidence is still on the shelf over in Pecore's offices."

"What am I looking for? Pecore's labeling is awful."

"You might find a plaster cast of a footprint. I was representing that young Native American, the one who died in jail, and they alleged to have found his footprint outside the kitchen window: a Nike tennis shoe, size ten.

"You have *nooo* idea how much I wanted to go to trial with that as their sole evidence that he had been on the property," said Lillie, her voice a buzz saw. "Do you have any idea how many men and boys wore size ten Nikes in those days? Molly's father was one."

"But the key piece of evidence was the pair of pajamas that Molly was wearing when she was found. I was told at the time that she had been sexually abused by the killer, and the proof was a semen stain found on her pjs. However, the physician who examined her found no signs of an assault. I've always felt it was possible the killer left those stains to divert the investigation, to hide his motive for killing her parents."

"Really," Lew asked. "What makes you think that?"

"It was a chicken-hawk murder. A gay revenge killing."

"Lillie," Osborne asked, stunned. "Are you sure?"

"After the boy's death, I did some detective work on my own. Molly's parents were in marriage counseling at the time. Her father wanted a divorce. He had decided he was bisexual and had fallen in love with a man. But he would never say who it was.

"I know this because I spoke with the minister who was counseling them. Unfortunately he's no longer alive. But Molly's aunt is, and, Chief Ferris, she knew about the marital problems. She can back up everything I'm telling you. Before you leave, I'll give you her phone number.

"That coupled with the violence against the wife convinced me. She was killed first, in the downstairs family room where she was ironing. Bludgeoned to death with a portable radio. Then the killer went up two flights to the bedrooms, where he took a baseball bat to the father and the son who were asleep in upstairs bedrooms. And—*and*," Lillie shook a finger, "the family dog was killed where it was sleeping on the floor near the boy's bed."

"So the family dog knew the killer," said Lew.

"That's right. I am convinced that the family was killed by the man with whom Molly's father was having an affair, and I'm damn sure that man is Jerry O'Brien."

Lew leveled a long look at Lillie. "How can you be so sure that he was the one?"

"I know someone who saw them together," said Lillie. "Unfortunately, this person—who is no longer alive, so I'm not violating my client's confidentiality—

was so frightened of Jerry that she refused to go to the police. She was just a girl at the time, working at the newspaper, and even later in life never a person with much confidence."

"You don't mean Sherry Peterson?" asked Osborne, remembering the small, slight woman who walked hunched over as if permanently expecting a blow. A woman so shy, she never spoke above a whisper. She'd lived with her elderly father and died within a few months of his death.

"Yes," said Lillie.

"About two years before she died, she came to me for legal advice. She'd been at the newspaper for ages, working in the accounting department, when she was accused of stealing. It was her supervisor who was the guilty party. He thought he could bully poor little Sherry into resigning so it would look like she was guilty. I got wind of what was going on and insisted she sit down with me—we got things straightened out."

"I'm sure you did," said Lew.

"One day, out of the blue, I asked Sherry if she had known Molly's father. The look on her face . . . *pure terror*. Knowing she trusted me, I pressed her on it. I promised I would tell no one. And I haven't until now.

"She told me that one night she had had to work late in the back office. Now, this was a week or so before the family was killed. She thought she was the only one in the building and was on her way to the bathroom when she heard voices. The door to Jerry's office was ajar, and all the lights were on. She couldn't help but see Jerry and Patrick together. This was a woman who had never seen men as lovers. She was shocked, she was frightened. Thank goodness, they did not see her.

"Then, when Patrick was murdered days later, she felt very confused and afraid. She kept that secret for all those years, never even told her father. I didn't do anything about it at the time because I knew Sherry could never testify in court. She wasn't mentally and emotionally capable of that." With a sigh, Lillie said, "If only Sherry hadn't been such an easily frightened little person. . . ."

Lew raised a hand. "It's not just Sherry—better police work might have changed things."

"Still can," said Lillie. "We need those pajamas, Chief. They may not have had DNA testing in those days—but we sure as hell do now."

twenty-three

If you swear, you will catch no fish.

—Anonymous

Erin was waiting in Lew's office when they got back to the courthouse. She stood up as they walked in.

"Hey, Dad, Chief Ferris, thank goodness. I was afraid you'd be late. Ready, Chief? Let's head out." Erin tossed her long blonde braid back and gave Lew a cheerful smile. "Look," she said, lifting an armful of flyers. "Got the van gassed up, these are ready, and it's a lovely evening." She headed for the door, then stopped.

"What?" she asked. "Don't tell me we're not going."

"I can't," said Lew. "Your father knows. I've got two major investigations going on and just got handed a third. A young woman's life is in danger. Spending time on a political campaign right now—I'm afraid I just can't justify it."

Erin looked at Osborne, then back at Lew. The cheeriness faded. "Okay . . . then I'll tell you what. I'll go myself and hand out these flyers. Urge people to vote for you. Dad, why don't you help me."

"No," said Lew. "I'm seriously considering withdrawing from the race. With the election less than six weeks away, it makes more sense to stop wasting my money and your time."

"But, Chief, the opposition—you've got it made. Those two young guys from Rhinelander don't have credentials close to yours. I'm sorry, but this is not smart. Look at the job. It pays twice as much, you will have the kind of operation that—that—you'll be less stressed out than you are with this podunk setup."

Lew threw her notebook on her desk. "This 'podunk setup' as you call it, Erin, is a job I happen to like, believe it or not. And right now, I have a lot of work to do."

"Give Lew some time to think it over, Erin," said Osborne, putting his arm around his daughter's shoulders. "Too much is happening right now.

"Oh, shit!" Erin thrust herself away from Osborne. As she left the room, she slammed the door behind her.

"Sorry, Doc, that's the way it is." Lew studied the list of messages that Marlene had left on her desk.

Osborne sighed. "I'll talk to Erin. She'll come around."

After a dinner of leftover chili that he pulled out of the freezer, Osborne sat out on his deck, eyes closed, thinking over the day's events. Mike, curled up next to his chaise lounge, was happy he was home. Knowing that Lew was in her office, up to her ears in paperwork, made Osborne feel guilty.

Five minutes after sitting down, he decided to get up. Through the leaves perforating his view of the sky, he could see popsicle-pink clouds overhead. He decided to let the sky win and headed down to the dock to practice casting with his fly rod.

With Mike alongside, he sauntered down to the water. He threaded the fly line, checked his leader and tippet, then tied on a small cork-bodied, frog-colored size ten popper he thought might appeal to a bluegill. He rollcast to get some line out. Then he backcast . . . and tugged.

"Great," he said, looking back at the baby oak he had just caught. "You know, Mike, this is not what I want to do right now."

Back up at the house, he called Erin. No one was home. He called Ray. No one there either. He left a message saying he hoped Ray could give him an address for Darryl Wolniewicz—but not to call after eleven. A wave of fatigue reminded him he'd gotten very little sleep the night before.

He went back onto the deck, back into his chaise, and picked up the *Loon Lake Daily News*. He read "Ask Hope." The subject of the day was how to properly make a contribution to a charity instead of sending flowers to a funeral—yet be able to notify the family of what you did without being tacky. He folded the paper and closed his eyes.

When the phone rang, he woke to darkness. The house was as dark inside as out, as he hurried for the kitchen and his cordless phone. He checked the wall clock— ten P.M.

"Doc," said Lew. "Sorry to bother you, but I just had a surprise visitor. Said she had to get something off her chest. Julia Wendt. Seems the nights that Kitsy said Julia was staying with her at her house? She wasn't.

Kitsy was behaving so strangely, Julia felt better spending her evenings up at the casino."

"By herself?"

"That's what she said. She said she returned when she was sure Kitsy had fallen asleep—only Sunday night she was not in her bedroom when Julia got back. I asked her if Kitsy had made any reference to the work she was doing for her mother. She said that Kitsy had indeed. She had been very upset and swore she hated her mother. Julia said she was feeling very uncomfortable around Kitsy right now."

"Is she still over there?"

"No. She's staying at the Claridge in Rhinelander."

"Well," Osborne asked, "what next? I don't suppose you've talked to Bunny DeLoye yet. She's likely to have seen some comings and goings, don't you think?"

"I hope to see her first thing in the morning."

"Any more news from Lillie?"

"No, but I checked to see if the GPS is working on that unit I gave Molly, and it appears she arrived safely back at Lillie's."

"I hope that means you can get a good night's rest."

"About ready to leave. I'll check Pecore's office for the evidence on the McBride case tomorrow. I'm too tired tonight. How's Erin, Doc? I'm afraid I was too abrupt."

"She'll recover. Now get a good night's sleep, will you please?"

"I promise. One last thing. Would you have the time to give that aunt of Molly's a call in the morning? She lives in Edina, Minnesota. Here's her number. . . ."

twenty-four

Every man has a fish in his life that haunts him.

—Negley Farson

Osborne woke to heaviness in the air. A stop-start patter of rain outside the bedroom window encouraged sleeping in. He resisted, pushed himself out of bed, and let Mike out the back door. Thankful that he had remembered to set the timer on the coffeemaker before going to bed, he poured a cup, then walked back to turn on the TV and check the weather channel.

As usual, the forecast appeared to be for another country, if not another continent. Sunshine was predicted in spite of the evidence outside the window: legions of surly clouds pressed in from the west, darkening the lake.

Osborne turned away from the window. This would be one of those northwoods days with rain moderating from heavy to pounding and back to heavy. The kind of day tourists cursed: twelve hours indoors face-to-face with your kids? God help us.

That made it Osborne's turn to curse. The families would head for town, swarming Main Street and the Loon Lake Market and letting their little stinkers scamper from the market over to Ralph's Sporting Goods and back again. Parents would lose patience and back their SUVs into one another in the parking lots: more work for the already stressed Loon Lake Police Department.

Osborne checked the time. Was seven-fifteen too soon to call someone you don't know? Hell, if they weren't up by now, they should be. He punched in the number for Molly's aunt.

A woman's voice answered immediately. "Hello, this is Georgia."

"Georgia Balczer? This is Dr. Paul Osborne from Loon Lake, Wisconsin. I'm calling on a matter that concerns your niece, Molly. Have I caught you at a bad time?"

A sudden intake of breath—"Molly! Is she all right?"

"She's fine—but we have a situation here. The head of our police department, Lewellyn Ferris, has asked me to check on a few details from the past."

"You're the police?" He hated the sound of worry crowding into her voice.

"Personally, I'm part-time. I retired from my dental practice up here several years ago and help out on occasion as a deputized officer—that's what I'm doing this morning, if you don't mind."

"Not in the least. You caught me as I was walking out the door for work, but take your time. Anything to do with Molly comes first. Tell you the truth, I've been worried ever since she told me she was returning to Loon Lake."

"Why is that?"

"You know her family was murdered years ago."

"That's one reason I'm calling."

"So much about that crime was unresolved. For me, anyway. I'm not sure Loon Lake is the place for Molly. You know my husband and I raised her."

"Yes. And you folks are familiar with the man she married?"

"*Ohhh*, yes. Jerry O'Brien. We're not happy about it either. Such an extreme age difference. Not to mention his connection to . . . well, to circumstances I'd always hoped Molly could put behind her."

"How well do you know Mr. O'Brien?"

"He was Molly's dad, Patrick's, best friend. And he's the one who found the bodies. Over the years, he's stayed in touch and has gone out of his way to look after Molly. . . ." She paused, then asked, "May I speak in confidence, Dr. Osborne? What I mean is, can I tell you some things that Molly doesn't know—and can you promise me this won't get back to her unless there is a very good reason for it?"

"I don't see why not," said Osborne.

"She doesn't know that Jerry paid the bills for her college and graduate school. We didn't ask—he volunteered—on the condition that she never be told."

"So the marriage surprised you?"

"To put it mildly. Dr. Osborne, do you have daughters?"

"Two."

"How would you feel if one married a man thirty years her senior—a man who had played such a role in her life, whether she knew about it or not? And she did this less than three months after being dumped by a young man her own age with whom she had been living with for two years?"

"I would think she acted on the rebound and made a

serious mistake. And you make O'Brien sound like a creep . . . frankly."

The line was silent, then Georgia said, "Well, nothing to do about it now."

"Georgia, does the name Lillie Wright ring a bell? The reason I'm asking is she has some strong opinions on Molly's situation—"

"Of course I know Lillie. The woman is a godsend. She got us through that terrible time, and she's been handling Molly's inheritance. She's the one who encouraged us not to sell her parents' house after it had stayed on the market so long that first time around. She told us the value of lakefront property would skyrocket and, boy, was she right. Molly has something now.

"Whatever Lillie says, pay attention. I still get goose bumps when I think of what she told us back then."

"Really?"

"Oh, yes. She knew from the beginning what was going to happen. It was eerie. You see, we got the news midmorning that terrible day and jumped right in our car. Within four hours, my husband and I were there to help with Molly."

"How was she when you got there?"

"Pretty calm. Remember, she was only three years old. As far as I know, she has no memories of that weekend—although we never brought it up either."

"This may be a difficult question," said Osborne. "We understand that Molly was sexually assaulted—"

"That's what they said at the time. But we had her examined when we got back here, and he found no indication of that. I'm an oncology nurse, Dr. Osborne. I know what to look for, and I saw no indication that

Molly had been hurt. So that was strange. But there were other things that didn't make sense."

"For example?"

"As you know, Jerry and Patrick worked together. Jerry ran the newspaper and after meeting Patrick at a newspaper convention, hired him to be the managing editor. So when Patrick didn't show up for work that Monday and no one answered the phone at their house, Jerry drove over there. That's when he looked through a window, saw my sister's body, and called the police.

"Now what I'm going to tell you next is what I was told by a young police officer who was standing outside the house when the bodies were found. He said two officers went in. They found the bodies, and they found Molly alive. Since Jerry was a friend of the family's, they decided to have him be the person to help with Molly. They asked him to wait outside the house, on the sidewalk leading up to the front porch.

"What was weird, said the young officer who was standing right beside Jerry, was that when they carried Molly out of the house, they set her down on her feet. She saw Jerry and ran towards him. He went down on one knee, held out his arms, and *made an awful face at her*."

"You're kidding."

"Twisted his face, the way you do when you want to scare someone."

"And Molly's reaction?"

"No one noticed. I asked the same question but no one was watching her—they were all waiting to see what was in the house. It was that one young police officer who couldn't believe what Jerry did.

"Think about it, Dr. Osborne. Why would you do

that to a child who has just been through a traumatic experience? Make a horrible face. I have never figured that out. By the way, that same police officer told me later that from where Jerry had said he was standing to look in the window—*you couldn't see Janet's body*."

"No one questioned that? Not the chief of police?"

"No, only that young man. In fact, he and Lillie Wright were the only two who felt that the police arrested the wrong person when they put that boy in jail."

"Do you remember the police officer's name?"

"If I did, it wouldn't help. He was shot and killed six months later. They found his body by his car out at a boat landing somewhere."

"Let's go back to Lillie for a moment," said Osborne.

"Yes. We first met with her two days after the bodies were found. We needed someone locally to help us with the legalities of the estate and Molly's guardianship.

"That's when she told us she was convinced it was a gay revenge murder. What she said next, I will never forget. Her exact words were: 'Some kid from the wrong side of the tracks will be charged, he'll die in jail before coming to trial, and the cops will clean off their desks.'"

"'And the cops will clean off their desks'?" Osborne repeated what she said. "I'm not sure what that means."

"Lillie said they would pin every outstanding assault-and-battery case on whoever it was. And that is exactly what happened."

"How do you think she knew?"

"When I asked her that, she said she'd seen enough

over her years practicing criminal law in Milwaukee and Madison. She also had no use for the man who was the chief of police at the time."

"Cynical old bird, isn't she."

"She knows people—too well."

"How did you feel when she said it was a gay revenge murder? Did that seem likely to you?"

Georgia sighed. "The 'gay' part did. My sister and I were close. She'd told me that Patrick wanted out of the marriage, and she told me why."

Georgia paused, "It was such a hard thing for Janet. You know they had only lived there seven months, so she knew no one, had no friends. She felt so angry, so humiliated. This was long before people understood bisexuality. I think if they were going through this today, she would have had a different attitude."

"So her husband was open about being in love with another man?"

"Yes, quite. He was leaving her to live with his lover."

"And did she know who this was?"

"No. He refused to tell her. Also, something else she told me—she was convinced he was having an affair with a woman, too."

"Any idea who that was?" asked Osborne.

"No. But when the police checked the phone records of calls going to their home that weekend, the last one was from a pay phone near the bowling alley. It was made Saturday night around eleven o'clock. People leaving the bowling alley said they saw a woman in the phone booth that night. Now, I heard from other people at the newspaper where he worked that Patrick seemed to spend quite a bit of time with one young woman reporter in particular. But that's as much as I know.

"Dr. Osborne, looking back now I see how Patrick was a very confused soul. But to be perfectly honest, my sister didn't help matters. She was not kind. It wasn't in her nature, for one thing, and then you shatter her life? Molly is not like Janet. She is not like my sister. She is her father's daughter—she looks like him, she even sounds like him at times."

"Georgia," said Osborne, "Lillie is convinced it was Jerry who murdered your sister and her family. She is afraid for Molly. Molly herself told us yesterday that his behavior towards her changed right after the marriage—in ways she finds so disturbing that she has moved out and is staying with Lillie."

"I'm driving over," said Georgia. "This sounds terrible."

"It's not good," said Osborne. "Chief Ferris is likely to reopen the murder case. We're hoping to find the evidence still in storage—that it hasn't been destroyed."

"Then two things that you should know," said Georgia, her voice shaking. "When Molly was questioned by the police the day after she was found—actually they had a child psychologist talk to her—all she could remember from that night was 'the nice man with the yellow hair.' Nothing about his face or whether he was short, tall, fat, or skinny—just the yellow hair. Made me think whoever it was wore some kind of a mask or a scarf around his face that didn't cover his head."

" 'The nice man with the yellow hair,' " said Osborne, writing down what she said.

"Yes, and the boy who was accused was Native American, dark-skinned with black hair. Jerry O'Brien, thirty years ago, was fair-skinned with reddish-blond hair.

"So she wasn't able to recognize a face or a voice?"

"No. Something else—and Molly doesn't know this—but on her fourth birthday she was sent a card that I felt was very threatening. It was sent by the killer, I'm sure."

"Do you remember what it said?"

"Not exactly. I remember the words were cut out of a newspaper. But I did save it. It's in our safe-deposit box with the rest of Molly's documents. The card and the envelope it came in are in a manila folder I haven't opened in years. Funny, I thought about it just recently, too, knowing all the advances with DNA."

"How easy is it for you to get to the bank and send that to us?" asked Osborne.

"I'll pick it up and drive it over myself. I'll need to make arrangements at the medical center, but I'll be in Loon Lake first thing tomorrow morning. You've got me worried."

twenty-five

The fishing was so good, I thought I was there yesterday.

—Dave Engerbretson

Osborne stood in front of his refrigerator, peering into the freezer section and feeling sorry for himself. After alerting Lew to expect Georgia the next morning, he had spent the day catching up with housekeeping and bills, then two hours at the vet, who'd had an emergency arrive minutes before Osborne was scheduled to have Mike vaccinated for Lyme disease.

They didn't get out of the animal hospital until after six o'clock. As Mike leaped into the back of the car, Osborne scanned the sky overhead. The air seemed thicker, if that was possible, the morning dark as dusk and the clouds overhead ready to burst—but no rain yet. It was now nearly seven, he was starving and he'd forgotten to think about food until just a few minutes ago.

He reached for a package wrapped in white butcher paper. Ground venison. Nope, take too long to thaw. A Lean Cuisine tuna casserole that Mallory had left behind. Not much of a meal for someone who'd skipped lunch. Two walleye he was saving for the highly unlikely evening when Lew might be free for dinner. And a Ziploc of frozen chili probably six months old, if not a year. He reached for the chili.

As he filled a saucepan with water for boiling, he could hear the wind bellow through the pines. He had just turned around to set the pan of water on the stove, when a voice out of nowhere shouted his name. Startled, he jerked the pan, spilling enough water to douse the gas flame.

"Lewelleyn, you scared me to death. When did you get here?"

"Just now," said Lew, bounding into the kitchen with a wide grin on her face. "Didn't you hear me drive up?"

"Not over that wind."

"Wind from west—west is best. I'm ready to go."

And she was—in khaki shorts, her favorite fishing shirt, a rain poncho tied around her waist, and her curls clamped down under her fishing hat. "You coming or not? Got sandwiches packed. Gotta get out there before the storm hits. Could not ask for better conditions . . .what's wrong?"

"I'm just a little taken aback is all. I assumed you'd be up to your ears in paperwork tonight. Any break in the McDonald murder?"

"Couple new developments that I'm thinking over. Tell you about it when we're in the boat—need your opinion. And you're right, a mountain of paperwork to be tackled . . . so what better time to duck out of the office?"

A rueful expression crossed her face. "I know I'm playing hooky but, Doc, I've said this before and I'll say it again: No matter how busy I am, grabbing an hour or two to fish doesn't hurt. The job always gets done. Whereas you and I both know we don't get perfect muskie conditions like tonight more than twice in a summer."

She was right. The hot days, the heavy overcast, the wind out of the west—no better time to fish the big "girls" than that first half hour of rain.

"You say you've got sandwiches?" Osborne threw the chili back in the freezer.

"Peanut butter and lettuce, some chips, couple sodas—we're set."

Ten minutes later, with the spray forcing them to put on their ponchos in spite of the heat, they were nearing the entrance to a stream emptying into Loon Lake that they had fished before. A short way up, the stream widened.

"Want to try this pothole?" asked Osborne, shouting over the wind. Lew nodded happily. He swung the boat towards a section he knew was like a nursery for the big fish. The water was only twenty-four to thirty-six inches deep and loaded with bullrush and sandweed, ideal for a predator lurking in ambush.

"Stay out a ways," said Lew. "I borrowed this fly rod from Ralph—need room to backcast."

"Okay," said Osborne, waiting to drop anchor until he saw her nod with approval.

"Casting into the wind?" asked Osborne, dubious. He sure hoped she wasn't expecting him to do the same. He had a tough time getting a fly out forty feet in perfect conditions.

"Oh yeah, I'll just double haul. You watch, Doc, it'll work fine."

He was happy to watch, hunger forgotten, as Lew uncased the rod. He knew from previous discussions that if she liked it—the first rod ever designed exclusively for fishing the freshwater "shark of the north"—she was planning to buy one, even if it did cost six hundred bucks.

What she didn't know was that he might beat her to it. He hoped to surprise her with the 9-foot 9-weight St. Croix Legend Elite along with a lightweight Ross Evolution reel—upon winning the election for sheriff. Assuming she would change her mind and not drop out of the race.

As she was threading her fly line up through the guides, Lew said, "Guess what Ralph told me today. . . ."

"I'm afraid to ask," said Osborne, waiting patiently for direction and sitting quite still. Since there was only one fly rod in the boat, he assumed he would be bait casting with his muskie rod.

"He said that fly fishermen are catching three times as many muskies as the guys bait casting. Do you believe that?"

"I believe he wants to sell expensive fly rods," said Osborne. He also believed that Ralph paid way too much attention to Lew. That the man was married made no difference. Osborne didn't like it, and he didn't like Ralph.

"Be kind, Doc," said Lew, with a teasing glance. "I think it's because you get better line control with a fly rod—you can get to the fish easier."

"I suppose he's got some custom fly line on there, too," said Osborne. "Wonder how much *that* costs?"

"I dunno," said Lew. "It's new from Cortland—Ghost Tip. It's an intermediate sink tip line, clear and tapered. Sixteen pound test class tippet. If it gets my fly down fast without spooking the fish, I don't care what it costs."

She reached into her tackle box and pulled out one of the longest streamer flies Osborne had ever seen. It was orange and brown and black with strands of gold flashing. And it made sense: if a trout fly has to imitate the insects trout are feeding on, then a muskie fly better imitate the fish on which the big girls are preying.

"Isn't that going to be tough to cast?" asked Osborne.

"Not with the double haul," said Lew, getting to her feet in the boat. "Double hauling makes casting with heavier rods and in tougher conditions *so* much easier. That's why I keep trying to get you to learn, Doc."

As she tied on the streamer, she said, "Bill Sherer up in Boulder Junction made this. Calls it a Sucker-colored Figure Eight. He customized this wire weed guard, too, so it ought to run smooth." She got to her feet in the rocking boat, faced the wind, and began stripping line from the reel.

"Wait, wait," said Osborne, struggling to keep his voice low. After all this effort, the last thing he needed was to make too much noise in the boat and scare off any fish lurking below. "What do you need me to do?" The wind had begun to throw pellets of rain at their faces.

"Oh, jeez, I'm sorry, Doc," said Lew with a light laugh. "I'm so excited—I forgot about you."

"Thank you!" He tried for a grumpy look. She leaned over and kissed him on the cheek.

"Okay, sweetie, tell you what. You take that surface mud puppy of yours, and you bait cast from where you are in the front there. It's your job to stir things up, and when we get one interested, I'll do my best to put the fly right in front . . . get it down where she can see it. We cast into the wind—both of us."

"Gotcha," said Osborne, checking to be sure he had his six-foot net and Boga Grip close at hand. Big muskies like to bite, and he had learned long ago to be ready with the Boga—forget the old "fingers in the gills" routine. Of course, all this was wishful thinking. The "fish of ten thousand casts" bore its nickname for good reason. But Osborne, like all dedicated muskie fishermen, never launched a cast without hope.

As he got to his feet, Lew tapped him lightly on the shoulder. "Doc," she said with a wide grin, the color high in her cheeks, "I feel lucky tonight. . . ."

Osborne chuckled, thinking: "Life doesn't get much better than this."

He threw his first cast. The lure was heavy enough to buck the wind for a high, long flight. Watching it fly towards the horizon, he noticed that the clouds overhead were roiling, much lower than when they had set off from the dock. The air was thick and green. Had to be ninety-five degrees. He was glad that he'd left Mike in the house where it was cooler.

He was on his twentieth cast when Lew gave a low shout: "Shadow!"

Sure enough, fifteen feet from the boat, a lunker was following his surface mud puppy as it whipped through the water. Keeping the rod tip down, he made a figure eight near the boat.

"Go for it," he said to Lew, who was busy stripping line. She started her backcast, her line hand pulling the line in on her power snap, then giving it back as the line unrolled backward. As she forward cast, her line hand pulled the line in on the power snap, this time giving it back as the line unrolled forward.

Osborne was mesmerized by the grace and physics of the double haul. Watching Lew's arms move in opposition, her body swaying in cadence to unheard music, he wondered if he could ever master the marvelous movements.

"You'll learn," she'd said after his first futile attempts. "One day it'll just click, and you'll dance the dance. That's when you'll know what makes me love fly-fishing."

"What makes you so beautiful," thought Osborne, oblivious to how hard the rain was falling. They were protected from the worst of the wind as the fishing boat rocked rhythmically over the waves. Lew was steady on her feet, her eyes fixed on the dark water and the shadow of a very large fish.

Lew teased again and again, arms in concert, each move flowing into the next, power snaps crisp and delicate. Down went the rod tip into the water each time her streamer neared the boat.

"She's staying with my fly, Doc," said Lew, holding her breath. "She's gonna take—"

With a splash and a swirl, the fish inhaled the streamer.

Osborne watched the line race from Lew's reel as the fish headed for the open water downstream. That's when he saw the funnel moving across Loon Lake in their direction.

"Tornado!" he screamed.

twenty-six

The end of fishing is not angling, but catching.

—Thomas Fuller

What happened next took less than five seconds: Osborne hauled at the anchor with both hands. Lew grabbed clippers from the tackle box at her feet and cut the line. Osborne yanked the cord on the outboard and had it full throttle just as Lew was shoving the fly rod onto the bottom of the boat.

A small clearing a hundred yards off was their only hope. If they were lucky, there'd be no hidden deadheads to stop them. As they got close to shore, Osborne gunned the motor one last time, yanked the outboard up, and shouted, "Hold on!" The boat hit the shore and ran up a good twenty feet onto the beach.

They were out and running. Osborne looked back to see the funnel veer slightly to the north. "This way, Lew," he said, grabbing for her hand. "Down!" They hit a basin of hillocks, swampy but low, and lay flat, hands covering their heads as the "train" roared by. Trees cracked, limbs crashed, and Osborne figured his boat of thirty years was long gone. But they were safe.

When the roar had moved on, he lifted his head just

as the rain poured down and lightning split the sky all around. Before he could say a word, Lew had jumped up and was running toward the boat, which had been blown over by the wind. "Don't worry about it," he shouted through the storm, but she was on her knees scrambling for something.

"Lew, we can't stay here."

"I know." She ran back toward him, her eyes sparkling through the rain as she held up the tackle box. "Sandwiches!"

"I see a path over here, let's see where it goes," said Osborne, pushing through tag alders heavy with wind. Black as the sky was, the path was easy to see in the rapid flashes of lightning. After five minutes, they found themselves in the parking area of a small tavern and raced for the door.

Inside all was dark, but there were people and voices. Cars were pulling over in the downpour, and more people ran in behind them. The bartender was just lighting a candle when he looked up and saw Osborne. "Oh, my gosh, Doc, were you out on the lake? You are one lucky son of a gun. Holy smokes! Who's this good-lookin' dame you got with you? At least she was good lookin' before you tried to drown her."

"Hey, we're alive," said Lew, shaking the water out of her hair. "Lew Ferris, pleased to meet you."

"Wally Gunderson," said the bartender. "Ol' Doc here was my dentist."

"Whew! We almost got nailed by a small tornado coming off the lake, Wally." Now Osborne recognized where they were: Wally's Place, beer, bait, and tackle. A cozy little tavern.

"So I been hearing from some of these other folks,"

said Wally, waving towards the room. Even in the dark Osborne could make out at least a dozen people who, judging from their wet hair and clothes, were also refugees from the storm.

"Sit right up here, people," said Wally to the room. "No power doesn't mean refreshments aren't available. Can't run the cash register, but I sure can open the fridge. What can I get you—first one's on the house."

Just as he spoke there was a loud crack, followed by a thudding crash. "Holy cow!" he said, running for the screen door. Everyone followed. "Who's driving that big red Expedition?" he asked.

"Oh, no, that's my dad's car! He doesn't know I got it," said a tall, lanky boy who couldn't have been more than sixteen. The kid looked past Wally and groaned.

"I think we better wait it out here, don't you?" asked Osborne as they walked back to the bar.

"Doc, we are lucky to be here."

"Hey, you two, what'll you have?" asked Wally as they sat down.

"Coke for me, and a Bud for the lady," said Osborne. Lew grinned. She reached into the tackle box and pulled out a sandwich for each of them, followed by a bag of tortilla chips and two apples.

"When was the last time peanut butter tasted so good?" she asked as they inhaled their food. "So, you want to hear what Bunny DeLoye told me this morning?"

"Of course."

"What she said is quite contrary to what I heard from Julia Wendt. Fact is, Julia did *not* leave the house any night last week. Bunny would know—her apartment is above the garage."

"So what you're saying is Julia—"

"Lied. Has deliberately made up a story to incriminate her good friend Kitsy. So I ask you, Doc, why would she do that?"

"From the look on your face, I have a hunch you've got the answer."

"Yes, sort of. When I got back from seeing Bunny DeLoye, I had several phone messages waiting for me. The first was from Hope McDonald's office manager. While they had no evidence in the Madison office of Hope receiving any threats from readers, she did pass along a tidy bit of information on Mr. Kelly. Seems his most recent hotel bill included a charge incurred at the hotel spa—a facial and a massage—for a party going by the name of Julia Wendt."

"I wonder if Kitsy knows—or has known."

"I doubt it. She's so angry with her father—that would have come out first thing. But the best news came from the least likely source." Lew took a big bite from her sandwich and chewed slowly, a twinkle in her eye. "Pecore."

"Pecore?"

"Yep. I thought it was hopeless asking him for the evidence from the McBride case. He found it. We have everything, including the baby's pajamas. Marlene pulled the files, which I'll look over first thing in the morning before the meeting with Molly and her aunt— and Lillie—tomorrow."

"I don't suppose you'll need me—"

"You better be there—you're one of the few people who's known Jerry O'Brien over the years. No, Doc, with the McDonald case still up for grabs, my budget may not be in the best of shape—but I can't let that get in the way of doing the job."

Wally, a kind, wide-faced man looked up from where he was washing glasses.

"Did I hear you mention Jerry O'Brien?"

"Yeah," said Osborne. "He's got a place around here, doesn't he?"

"Across the road on Little Moccasin," said Wally, drying his hands on a towel, then leaning forward over the bar. "Keeps his boat in my marina. Uses it to go back and forth 'cause he owns all the property on the point. Takes an hour to get there by county road, maybe ten minutes by boat."

"Friend of yours?" asked Lew. "Nice guy?"

"Oh, no, no friend. Just a patron. Strange one, that guy. Wouldn't you say so, Doc?" Osborne nodded his head. "Yep, scared the bejesus out of my kids years back. Nearly had to put 'em in therapy."

"You're not serious?" asked Osborne. "He frightened your children? How did that happen?"

"You gotta hear it from my wife," said Wally. "It's her story. Cindy!" He hollered down the bar to a short, trim woman who had been helping him serve. "Cindy, come over here for a minute."

Cindy finished handing a customer a beer, then walked towards her husband, wiping her hands on her jeans. "What's up?"

"Cindy, you know Dr. Osborne—"

"Of course I do. And I know Chief Ferris, too. You folks got caught in the storm, I take it." Cindy had a wide smile and cheekbones to match under a thatch of salt-and-pepper hair.

"We were just talking about Jerry O'Brien, and I

was saying how he scared the dickens out of our kids—
but you tell it better'n I do."

Cindy looked around as if to be sure Jerry O'Brien
wasn't standing behind her. "Really? You want me to
dredge all that up? It's not like he hurt anyone, y'know."

The noise in the bar had settled to a low hum. The
rain was less thundering, and no one was crowding the
bar. Cindy put her elbows on the bar and leaned in toward Osborne and Lew.

"This happened maybe fifteen or sixteen years ago.
Our boys were eight and ten, and we owned a couple of
lots over near the point. Sold 'em since, but there were
real nice blueberries on our land that abutted
O'Brien's.

"To keep the boys busy one day, I sent 'em over to
pick berries, and they took the dog along. Well, the dog
disappeared as dogs do, and the boys went into the
woods after her. Wouldn't you know she'd head
straight for Jerry's trash? So the boys find themselves
walking onto his property, and Jerry is out in the side
yard, but he doesn't see the boys."

"Tell 'em what he was wearing," said Wally from
where he was leaning back against the counter, arm
crossed, listening to his wife.

Cindy turned to give him a dim eye. "Wally? You
want to tell the story, or you want me to?" Wally raised
both hands in submission.

"The boys had started to run after Ginger but
stopped when they saw Mr. O'Brien lying in a lawn
chair sunning himself . . . in women's underwear. Not a
swimming suit, mind you—but women's underwear.
The boys described it as shiny silk. They didn't know
what to think—and it scared them. So now the dog is

running down to the water, but they don't dare let O'Brien see them hiding in the woods."

"Cindy's brother is gay," said Wally.

"Jeez, Wally, let me finish, will ya?" asked his wife. "So they come home without the dog, crying, and I am especially worried because, yes, my brother is gay, and I don't want the boys to have the wrong idea. Like I don't want them to think their uncle is weird or whatever.

"So we talk, and I try to explain to the boys that we all grow up differently and there's nothing wrong with that. And I do my best to help them understand that some men may want to wear women's clothing—but that doesn't mean their uncle does.

"I guess," Cindy paused, "they loved their uncle and had no image of him doing anything like that, which was a very bizarre sight for the boys. Now, I don't know if my brother cross-dresses or not, but if he does, that's his business. To this day, our sons love and respect their uncle—and have, I don't think, ever associated him with what they saw that day."

"How did you explain it?" asked Lew.

"Thank you for asking," said Cindy. "In fact, I didn't at first. I called a friend of mine from college who's a psychotherapist and asked her what to say. She suggested I explain to the boys that some people need softness in their lives. That maybe Mr. O'Brien had an experience early in his life that made him want to touch and feel soft, pretty things. Sounds wacky but it worked. The boys settled down. Instead of being frightened, they felt sorry for Jerry."

"So what you're saying is Jerry O'Brien forced *you* into therapy," said Lew with a chuckle.

"At least I didn't have to pay for it," said Cindy. "You want to know how fast we put that land on the market? The next day."

"Any more encounters with O'Brien?" asked Osborne. "Did he know the boys saw him?"

"Heavens, no," said Wally. "But he is one odd duck, I'll tell ya. Keeps to himself like you wouldn't believe. In all these years, I've never seen him take anyone else out to his place by boat, and he's back and forth all the time. What about you, Cindy? You ever see him with other people?"

"No, but he's always pleasant," said Cindy. "We run a small business down by the water. You know, some bait and staples like milk and bread. He'll stop in for things but never says much."

"You know," said Osborne, "that's Jerry all around. He ran that newspaper for years but now that you mention it, he's not very social. I can't think of a time I've seen him at a Friday fish fry. Can't be Catholic, I've never seen him at Mass."

"We're Methodists—and we've never seen him there," said Cindy.

"He's not a member of Kiwanis," said Wally.

"Here's what's really weird," said Cindy. "He never comes to our lake association meetings. Now for the investment in lake frontage that he's got, you'd think he'd at least show up for that. We're not talking social—we're talking money!"

twenty-seven

But what is the test of a river? "The power to drown a man," replies the river darkly.

—R.D. Blackmore

It was as if the tornadoes that swept through the north-woods were a figment of the imagination. The morning was brilliant with sunshine, and the sky so clear it turned the lake cornflower-blue. The water was still—not a breeze blemished its innocence. Only the tree limbs and swatches of pine needles littering Osborne's backyard bore testament to nature's bad behavior the night before.

To his relief, the boat had not been damaged, even though an ancient white pine less than five feet away was yanked and heaved with enough violence to leave only a gaping wound where its roots had been.

With Lew helping, he was able to right the boat, slide it across the sand, and back into the water. The outboard chugged into action with the first pull. But it was midnight when they reached his dock.

The effect of the adrenaline rush from the night before lingered as fatigue, which Osborne struggled to shake as he drove into town the next morning. The sluggish sensation lifted as he caught sight of the old courthouse dome, its Tiffany glass sparkling in the sun.

Lew's office was buzzing. Lillie was there along with Molly's aunt who had arrived and was seated in a chair next to Molly, with whom she was deep in conversation. The elderly lawyer, dressed in something black and flowing, refused to sit. She stood toward the back of the room, behind Molly, listening, watching. That body might be eighty-seven years old, thought Osborne, but not the eyes. Lillie's eyes were exceptional: curious, wise, and young.

Lew was behind her desk and up to her elbows in two cardboard boxes. The flaps were open, and she was bent over the contents. Scrawled across each of the boxes was one word: MCBRIDE.

"Dr. Osborne," said Molly, standing up as he entered the room, "I'd like you to meet my aunt, Georgia Balczer."

"Yes, we spoke on the phone," said Osborne, extending his hand to a butterball of a woman. Georgia was a good six inches shorter than her niece, with markedly different coloring: freckles, blue eyes, and strawberry-blonde hair. Quite a contrast to Molly's olive skin, dark eyes, and brown hair. Molly had to be one of those daughters who look like their fathers. The only resemblance Osborne could see was a soft kindness around the eyes.

"I haven't been able to sleep since we spoke," said Georgia. "I rushed to the bank right after your phone call and was able to find that card right away. Made arrangements at work so I could drive over late last night. Chief Ferris has the card and the envelope."

"I had copies made of what's written inside," said Lew, looking up. "Lillie, would you mind handing these out?"

"Not in the least," said Lillie, reaching for the copies.

"Before we talk about that, may I say something?" asked Molly. Her voice was even but Osborne noticed, now that she held a sheet of paper, that her hands were trembling.

Lew, who had found whatever it was she was searching for in the box, moved the boxes to the side and sat down, saying, "Go right ahead, Molly. By the way, I'm happy to see you're keeping that cell phone with you. Hope you've read the directions on how it works."

"Oh, yes. Got it right here." Molly pointed to a well-worn navy blue backpack at her feet. "Keeping it on all the time, just like you said."

"I noticed," said Lew, with a slight smile. "Marlene ran the software on our system around eight o'clock last night—checking locations on me, Todd, Roger, and you, Molly. Showed you about three miles southeast of town. At your parents' place—well, yours now, right?"

"Yes. Lillie and I drove out there last night. I don't know if I told you, but I hired a crew to clear the area around the house because it was so overgrown. You couldn't even see the lake from inside.

"When we drove up last night, it was like it used to be. Wide open with a few trees here and there, just like it looks in some family photos I have. And there's this one tree off the back patio that has this pretty little wooden bench encircling it. Used to be painted white. The minute I saw it I remembered. . . ."

Molly dropped her face into her hands. The room was quiet.

"You don't have to do this if it's too painful," said Georgia.

"No, I want to. It—it helps, really." Molly took a deep breath. "When I saw that bench, it was like a trigger. Everything came back. Everything I've not been able to remember came back: my mother's face, my dad, my little brother. All of a sudden I felt like they were there." A sob caught in Molly's throat.

"I just . . . I felt like I could hear them, I could see them."

"When you say 'everything,' do you have any recollection of . . . that night?" said Lew.

"Less a memory than a dream," said Molly, her voice stronger. "And I've been thinking about this ever since." She gave a weak laugh. "I have this vision of a giant. A tall gray giant with yellow hair, taller than our house. He keeps walking toward me and I'm afraid, I try to hide under my covers."

"So you're in your bed," said Lew.

"I guess so. I try to hide but he's so close—I can smell him. I wait for him to hurt me, but he doesn't—he's just . . . nice. Then he goes away, and there's a door. I want to get out. I'm trying so hard to open the door, but I can't reach the knob, and I keep crying for my mother."

"Molly was locked in her bedroom that entire weekend," said Lillie. "A blessing given what happened in that house."

"The other thing I remembered is this smell," said Molly. "Now I know why, when I was around Jerry when I first arrived here, I felt so comfortable. This is

back when he was going out of his way to be nice—
before the marriage. His smell had this weird effect on
me: He smelled *safe*. It's a funny smell—like a mix of
body odor and aftershave or something. Very pun-
gent."

"He does wear a strong cologne," said Osborne. "I
noticed it whenever he was in the dental chair."

"Odd how the mind works," said Lew. "You're saying you've had no memories of your family before seeing that bench last night?"

"Yeah, it's like my life started around age six. I've
had no memories of anything happening before that."

"This so-called birthday card was sent to Georgia's
home on the occasion of Molly turning four," said Lillie, striding back and forth and gesturing as if she was
in front of a jury. "Eighteen months after the murders.
And, may I remind you, *after* the alleged killer had
been arrested and so conveniently committed suicide
while in jail." Lillie paused. "Molly, are you okay with
this?"

The young woman nodded. "Ever since I saw that
bench, I feel like a weight has been lifted. Now I want
to know everything. *Everything*. This might sound
strange, but I feel good. It's like I'm getting my life
back."

"Okay, then," said Lillie, opening the manila folder
and holding it out so they could all see the front of the
card, which was decorated with a cake and four can-
dles.

"Please—under no circumstances should anyone
touch that card or the envelope," said Lew, reaching for
the folder. "It goes to the lab for DNA testing this

morning. Lillie, would you read from your copy what it says inside?"

Lillie gave a quick glance to be sure she had everyone's attention, then read, " 'Happy Birthday, little Molly. You could have been mine, little one. You should have been mine, little one. I have a gift for you today, little Miss Molly. I promise that someday we'll be together. Someday we'll die together.'

"And it's signed, 'Daddy's special friend.'

" *'Someday we'll die together,'* " said Lillie.

"When I read that, I took it as a threat," said Georgia. "Very, very upsetting."

"Georgia, we're lucky you kept the envelope it came in," said Lew. "With luck it'll have traces of saliva from the person who sent it."

"Yes, and now you have the pajamas," said Lillie. "How soon can we have the DNA tests run?"

"Wausau has agreed to bump us up and give me a twenty-four-hour turnaround," said Lew. "But what we need before we send the evidence to the lab is a sample from Jerry O'Brien. Molly, do you have something we can use?"

"Lillie asked me that before," said Molly, "and I've looked through all my things, but I'm afraid I don't."

"No strands of hair, no personal items that he might have used, anything he might have left skin cells on?"

"No, I'm sorry," said Molly. "I've checked everything."

"How 'bout a toothbrush?" asked Georgia. "Maybe you could grab his toothbrush."

"He uses an electric one," said Molly. "Guess I could sneak in and take it."

"Does he floss?" asked Osborne.

"Twice a day."

"Probably flushes it down the toilet," said Georgia, "that's what I do."

"No. He puts it in the wastebasket under the bathroom sink."

"Are you serious?" asked Lew. "All we need is a few strands of that dental floss. That could be an excellent secondary source."

"I know where he hides a key," said Molly. "And every day he leaves the house at ten A.M. to walk downtown for the *Wall Street Journal* and the *Chicago Tribune*. I could run in this morning and grab some. What time is it?"

"Nine . . . twenty-two," said Lew. "Okay, everyone. Let's have Molly do that—then Roger can take everything down to Wausau. Now, Molly, I'll get you a pair of latex gloves and an evidence bag. We want to be sure there's no contamination."

"Molly," said Georgia, after Lew left the room. She had been sitting with her arm around Molly's shoulders. "I've been meaning to ask you—how did Mr. O'Brien take it when you said you were leaving him?"

"I don't know. I never told him directly. I just packed my stuff and left when he wasn't home."

"Did you leave a note?"

"Yes, but all I said was I wanted to move into my own place and have some time to think. He knows I've been cleaning up my folks' house."

"But I refuse to let her stay out there all by herself," said Lillie.

"Thank goodness," said Georgia. "Where does he live? If it's almost nine-thirty, shouldn't you be on your way?"

Lew walked back into the room as she was speaking. "Here, put this in your backpack," she said, handing Molly a packet with gloves and an evidence bag.

"Molly's got a couple minutes before she needs to leave," said Osborne. "O'Brien's house is just two blocks from here. Lew, do you want me to drive her over?"

"If you would, Doc. I have a few more questions for Lillie and Georgia—"

"Excuse me, Chief Ferris," said Molly, checking her watch. "While I wait, could I take a quick look at those case files?"

Lew didn't answer. She glanced over at Lillie who shook her head.

"That's not a good idea, Molly," said Lew. "The photos from the crime scene are pretty disturbing. Wouldn't you rather remember your mom and your dad and your little brother as you do now?"

"Those files will serve no purpose other than to give you nightmares, young lady," said Lillie.

Molly looked back and forth between Lillie and Lew. "It's not like I haven't worked seven years in the news business. I've seen dead bodies before. I can handle it. I told you—I want to know *everything*." Still Lew made no move to give her what she wanted.

"Lillie," Molly pleaded, turning in her chair to face the old woman, "you're the one who told me you live by the Golden Rule—'Do onto others as you would have them do onto you.' I want to know what was done unto me. That's all."

Lew took one of the cardboard boxes and walked over to set it down by Molly's chair. The file with the photos must have been clearly marked because Molly pulled it out first. As she opened the file, Georgia turned away, one hand over her eyes. "I can't see those again," she said.

The room was quiet as Molly studied each of the black-and-white photos, her face stoic. Several times she checked her watch and, when she was finished, she placed the file back in the box. "The thing about nightmares," said Molly, a calm resolve in her voice, "they don't lie. Dr. Osborne, are you ready to drive me over?"

twenty-eight

They may the better fish in the waters when it is troubled.

—Richard Grafton

Osborne parked midway down the block behind a pickup truck belonging to a lawn crew working on the same side of the street as O'Brien's house. The neighborhood was older with two- and three-story wood frame houses dating from the 1920s. Set back from the sidewalk and framed with picket fences and generous lawns, each home had a detached garage backing onto an alley.

"Keep your head down until I see him leave," said Osborne over his shoulder to Molly, who was crouched low in the backseat. They didn't have long to wait.

On the dot of ten, Jerry O'Brien came down his front stairs and along the walkway through his front yard to the sidewalk, where he turned right and headed off in the direction of downtown Loon Lake. He walked with his feet slightly splayed, shoulders back, head high. Watching him, it struck Osborne for the first time in all the years he'd known O'Brien that from some angles he could be mistaken for a tall, big-boned woman. It was how he carried himself.

Once he had turned the corner, Molly jumped out through the car door and started for the house. "Wait," said Osborne, lowering the passenger-side window. "Don't forget the the evidence bag! You need those gloves."

"Oops." Molly skidded to a halt and returned to grab her backpack, slinging it over her right shoulder. Back she ran toward the house, stopping at the front stoop where she bent down, right hand feeling under a Japanese yew. In less than a minute, she had the house key in hand and was letting herself through the front door, closing it behind her.

Osborne waited. He checked his watch. Molly had said Jerry usually took about forty-five minutes to get the papers. He always stopped to have one cup of coffee at the nearby coffee shop, taking twenty minutes or more to peruse the front pages before heading home.

Osborne looked off to his left. Two mothers with toddlers in strollers were ambling down the street across from where he was parked. He recognized one as a friend of Erin's and gave a friendly wave.

When he looked back to see if Molly had come out yet, he was stunned to see Jerry jogging back down the sidewalk towards the house. As he ran, he kept checking the pockets of his khakis, front and back, then his shirt pocket: he must have forgotten his wallet. At the yew, he bent to reach for his house key. Osborne watched, breath held, as O'Brien ran his fingers around the low shrub, searching.

Frustrated, he stood, brushed the dirt off his hands, ran up the front stoop, and tried the front door as if he expected it to be locked. But it opened. He disappeared inside, leaving the front door ajar.

Osborne wasn't sure what to do. He waited, thinking Molly was smart enough to come up with some excuse. Heck, she could say she'd forgotten something. He waited, deciding that if she didn't come out within five minutes, he'd better go in. It was the longest five minutes he could remember.

Running up the front stoop, Osborne pushed at the door. It opened farther. Molly was standing at the end of the hall, her eyes wide with an expression he didn't recognize until it was too late. Then, as if it was happening to someone else, he heard rather than felt the crack behind his right ear. The room went black.

As he came to, he got a whiff of Jerry O'Brien odor that was so strong he thought he would gag. "Doc, you okay?" Lew was kneeling over him. "Don't move till the paramedics get here."

"Oh, my head," said Osborne, pushing himself up on both arms.

"O'Brien clocked you a good one," said Ray from where he was standing behind Lew.

"Ray, *ooh*, ouch. Hey, how did you get here?" asked Osborne, relieved he could put one word after another.

"I knew from Lew that you would be in her office this morning. I was on my way in to show you and Lew my photos from the fishing clinic, when she came rushing out. Got some great shots of you, Doc—without a lump on your head."

"That's enough, Ray—I want Doc to keep still." Lew's hands felt good on his back. "You sure you want to sit up, Doc? You probably have a slight concussion. I called an ambulance. Be here any second."

"Oh, gosh, no," said Osborne, struggling first to his

knees, then to his feet. "No ambulance, Lewellyn." He saw the worry in her eyes. "Really, I'll be fine."

That wasn't exactly true. He felt a little woozy, and his head hurt like hell. He reached back over his right ear. A lump was forming. He saw now that he had fallen against an oak coat rack, pulling it down with him and landing with his head on one of O'Brien's jackets.

"Ouch. How long have I been out?"

"Maybe twenty minutes. He got you with this," said Lew, holding up an antique fishing gaff made of solid oak with a hook on one end. "Gave you a good clout. We're lucky he didn't do worse."

Ray slipped an arm under one elbow. "You sure you're okay, Doc?"

"How'd you know to find me here?" asked Osborne, feeling steadier by the moment.

"I was showing Lillie the locator software on the computer—how we could keep track of Molly. When her signal started moving in the wrong direction, I knew something was wrong. The two of you should have been headed back to my office and not—"

"Molly! Where *is* Molly?" asked Osborne, realizing that Lew had chosen to help him first.

"Settle down, Doc. We'll find her. Got an APB out on O'Brien's Jeep, though it took a little too long to get his vehicle license number. Before we lost the signal, I could see they were headed east."

"Lost the signal?" asked Osborne. "Why would that happen?"

"Probably driving a back road with heavy cover—" said Lew.

"Or he found her phone and threw it out the window," said Ray.

"We don't know—but if you're sure you're okay, then Ray and I are—" An ambulance siren sounded in the background.

"Lew, I'm going to be fine," said Osborne. "If you had O'Brien heading east, chances are he's taking her to that cabin of his."

"Why would he do that?" asked Ray. "Doesn't he know we'd look there first?"

"He thinks Molly is on her own," said Lew. "He doesn't know she's spoken to anyone. He certainly doesn't know that she went to Lillie for help."

"Doc, let's get moving," said Lew. "I'll alert the paramedics that we don't need them. I've got Todd standing by in his cruiser waiting for the minute we get Molly's signal back. Meantime, let's go for O'Brien's cabin."

"The quickest way we can do that is by boat from Wally's marina on Little Moccasin," said Osborne. "Don't you think, Ray?"

"Yep. Otherwise you got at least a half-hour drive."

As they climbed into Lew's cruiser, she radioed Marlene. "Any news? Good, I was hoping to hear you say that. Okay, Marlene, I'll stay off my cell phone in case I hear anything from Molly. Let's hope she knows how to use the push-to-talk feature on that thing."

Turning on the siren and pressing the accelerator, Lew said, "They picked up Molly's signal a few minutes ago—just like we thought—Little Moccasin Lake. Todd's taking the road in."

twenty-nine

This is night fishing . . . a gorgeous gambling game in which one stakes the certainty of long hours of faceless fumbling, nerve-racking starts, frights, falls, and fishless baskets against the off chance of hooking into . . . a fish as long and heavy as a railroad tie and as unmanageable as a runaway submarine.

—Sparse Grey Hackle (Alfred Miller)

Wally was standing on the marina dock, a five-gallon can of gasoline in one hand, and a look of surprise on his face as Osborne and Lew ran towards him. Ray was still unfolding his frame from the backseat of the cruiser.

"What is this? No sooner do I tell you two that Jerry O'Brien never has visitors than—whaddaya know? This morning he shows up with a woman. And now *you're* back. What's goin' on?"

"A young woman? Tall, dark hair?" asked Lew.

"Couldn't tell you exactly. Dark hair for sure, but all I could see was the back of her head. I was over in the bar when I heard someone drive up. By the time I stepped outside, the boat was pulling away from the dock. Fastest I've ever known that guy to move."

"We need a boat, Wally," said Osborne. "Police business." Wally's genial expression faded.

"Hope it's nothing I said. Didn't mean to get the guy in trouble. That all happened years ago—"

"Nothing to do with you, Wally," said Lew. "We need a boat."

"Take what you want. They're all gassed and ready." He waved a hand at six small fishing boats with ten-horsepower outboard motors, tethered to the dock. On the nearby shore were two kayaks and an overturned canoe. Paddles were stacked against a tree.

Ray stood off to one side, hands in the pockets of his khaki shorts, studying the lake. Off in the distance were three fishing boats and one inboard towing a water-skier.

"You fish this lake, Ray?" asked Lew.

"Oh, yeah, got a great sandbar for bluegills. Now if that's O'Brien's place out there," he said pointing to a peninsula on the northwest side of the lake, half-hidden by a small island, "then I think it's just as well we take a canoe—quieter. Otherwise, we'll end up having to cut the motor and row anyhow. Doc, you and I can pad-dle fast. Chief, we'll put you in the middle."

A chirping sound from Lew's waist caused the three men to turn and stare. Unbuttoning a small leather case slung alongside the holster for her gun, Lew pulled out a bulky cell phone identical to the one she'd given Molly. She raised a hand as she looked at the small screen in the handset, listened for a brief moment, then hit a button and held the phone out in front of her. "Caller ID on here shows it's Molly—I'll put her on speaker so we can all hear. . . ."

But it wasn't only Molly on the phone. As they listened another voice, high and reedy, a voice Osborne recognized, was heard: Jerry O'Brien. A Jerry O'Brien who appeared to be unaware he was on a conference call—that everything he had to say was being transmitted across the open water, the sound of his voice as clear as Little Moccasin Lake.

"All I want from you is *why*? And you don't need that gun, Jerry. I'm not going anywhere. I don't even know where we are."

Unlike O'Brien's, Molly's voice was muffled as if from a distance. Later, they would learn that as she was shoved through the door into the cabin, she had stumbled and fallen. In the midst of picking herself up, she managed to unzip her backpack wide enough to reach in and press the push-to-talk button on the phone, hoping that Lew—wherever she was—might hear.

"What do you want to know? Why I killed your parents? Or why I plan to finish what I started?"

"I saw what you did to my mother. Why did you have to be so brutal?"

"Can you hear okay?" asked Lew, holding the phone out as Ray and Osborne turned over the canoe and slid it into the water. "I've got the volume up as loud as it'll go." At the concern on Osborne's face, she said, "Don't worry, Doc, they can't hear anything from this end. She'd have to click off to hear me." Lew grabbed two paddles, which she cradled in one arm, keeping the phone held out in front of her.

But the phone was quiet. Lew checked to be sure it was on.

"Please, Molly, please keep him talking," said Ray,

climbing into the backseat of the canoe. Wally held it steady as Lew and Osborne got in.

Still no sound from the phone.

"C'mon, Molly, you've got to keep him going till we get there," said Lew, both hands tight on the phone. "Maybe she's saying something and we can't hear. . . ."

As Wally got ready to give the canoe a shove into deeper water, Lew said, "Wally, as fast as you can, call Marlene at the station, tell her where we are. Tell her to radio Todd to hold off on approaching O'Brien's property until he hears from me."

"Got it," said Wally as he heaved them forward toward the peninsula.

Osborne and Ray thrust their paddles deep, stroking fast. "What do you think, Ray?" asked Osborne. "Ten minutes to reach that peninsula?"

Before Ray could answer, they heard Molly's voice.

"Someone told me you killed my mother out of revenge. Revenge for what?" asked Molly. "You were the one breaking up the family."

"Your mother was a shrill, selfish bitch. She didn't deserve your father. And the things she said to him about me were . . . not very nice."

"What you said to me about my mother that night you locked me in the basement. Those were not *nice* words, Jerry."

"Careful, Molly. You're starting to sound like your mother."

"So? You brought me here for a reason. You said you plan to finish what you started. But why didn't you do away with me when you wiped out my family? What made you stop?"

"I meant to. I had every intention, but when I walked into your room and found you in your bed so scared, you put your arms up, and you were so happy to see me. You trusted me and . . . I made a mistake leaving you alive. Did you ever get that birthday card I sent?"

"No."

"Your aunt never told you about it?"

"No. When did you do that?"

"Good girl," said Lew. "Anything to keep him talking. . . ."

The phone was silent for a few beats, then O'Brien spoke. "Your mother died the way she did because she ruined things. Your father and I loved each other. I don't know if you can understand that. We could have had a good life together. But somehow she convinced him to stay. Some *lie* she told."

"You don't know that. My father loved her first. Maybe through all the marriage counseling, through all their fights over you—maybe they found they had something between them still. I mean—we were a *family*."

"All I know," Jerry's voice took on a monotone, "is that when I looked in the basement window that night and saw your mother doing her ironing, looking so goddamned self-satisfied—she was humming, for Christ's sake!—I knew right then it was she who ruined it all."

"Are you saying that at the last minute, my dad changed his mind? He and my mom weren't going to divorce?"

"That's what he told me when I called that night. We were supposed to leave on a business trip that Monday.

He said he wasn't going, that he was resigning from the paper."

"And so you killed them."

A low chuckle. "I have a way of going off sometimes."

"What you did to my mom—"

"Stop talking about her. She was a horrible woman."

Silence. Then Molly's muffled voice again, "She might have been horrible to you, but she was my mom." She sounded on the verge of tears.

"I should have been your mother."

Again, a long silence. Osborne wondered where Molly was finding the strength to keep going.

"I—I . . . how could that be?"

"Your parents should have divorced, your mother should have gone her way—I was giving her a lot of money. Then your father and I would have raised you and your brother. Your aunt must have told you why your father was leaving your mother: *he loved me*."

"I was three years old when it all happened. I've never known this story. Jerry," Molly asked, "why on earth did you marry me? I mean, what were you thinking—"

"I've always had a hunch you might come back to this town. And when you did, and I first saw you, all I could think about was how much you remind me of your father. You sound like him, you have his mannerisms—it's uncanny. I thought maybe . . . but you're just like your mother in so many ways, too, and that's why—that's why—"

"That's why this has to happen, is that what you're trying to say?"

"Not sure. Not sure about what I'm trying to say. But I'm damn sure about what I plan to do."

"And you'll get away with it, too. Just like that poor Indian boy who was accused of the murders and committed suicide—"

"That wasn't my fault. The cop in charge back then was so sure he had the right suspect." O'Brien laughed. "He made it so easy. He came up with all this evidence—none of which made any sense—but no one questioned him."

"I was told there were semen stains on my pajamas. But you didn't really hurt me, did you?"

"You were a little girl—of course I didn't hurt you."

"Then why—"

"Once I decided to leave you alive, I thought it would be a good idea if the authorities thought they were looking for a rapist. Worked. That's what prompted the cop to nail that kid—he had a record of assaulting women.

"Doesn't it amaze you, Molly, how murder is so easy? Look at today—no one knows you're here. When you don't show up in town, everyone will assume you've left me, that I'm the lonely, abandoned old man who should've known better. Say, want something to eat?"

"Something to eat?" Molly sounded incredulous.

"Yeah, I'm hungry, and I've got a few more things I want to say. I'm in no rush. I've waited years for this." The tone of O'Brien's voice caused the hair to rise on the back of Osborne's neck. They were closing in on the peninsula, and none too soon.

"See the island off the point," said Ray in a low

voice. "I think we should circle around that and approach from the far side so he doesn't see us coming."

Osborne nodded.

"I don't care for anything to eat, thank you. I don't feel very well. Would you mind if I used the bathroom?"

"All right—but don't lock the door. I don't need any funny business, like you locking yourself in there."

"Oh, no. I just—feel a little sick right now."

A sound of shuffling. Then footsteps closer to the phone. Osborne imagined O'Brien had enough common courtesy not to follow Molly all the way into the bathroom.

At least a minute went by. "What are you doing in there?" asked O'Brien.

From far away they could hear Molly say, "Just opening the window for a little air. One minute, okay?"

The canoe was nearing the island. They were about a hundred yards out from the dock fronting O'Brien's shoreline. The cabin, situated on a rise, was visible from the water.

"Molly?" Footsteps, then O'Brien's voice sounding distant. "Molly—"

The sound of a door slamming, then a string of expletives. "Molly? Molly!" His voice could barely be heard.

"I'll bet she went out that window!" said Ray. "I sure as hell would have."

A sharp bark from the shore. "He's shooting at her!" said Lew, reaching for her gun. She fired twice into the air, then shouted. "Loon Lake Police! Put down your gun, O'Brien."

"Careful, Chief. We're next," said Ray, swinging the canoe towards the island as Osborne stroked as fast as he could.

"I figured that," said Lew. "Anything to give her time to get away."

"He sees us," said Osborne, catching a glimpse of a figure standing outside on the cabin deck. "Heads down—and pray." They heard the bark of the rifle even as the bullet slammed into the canoe.

"Anyone hurt?" asked Osborne. Two more strokes, and they would have cover.

"No, but the boat's sinking," said Lew as water rushed in through the holes where the bullet had passed through the sides of the aluminum canoe.

"Thank the Lord that guy's a lousy shot," said Ray. "Hold on, we're close enough to the island, we'll make it."

"Yeah? Lot of good that does us," said Lew. "How do we get from the island to shore?"

thirty

Used trout stream for sale. Must be seen to be appreciated.

—Richard Brautigan

"Shallow here. We can wade," said Ray, letting himself over the side of the boat. Osborne and Lew followed, anxious to keep the canoe from sinking farther.

"If you two will get this canoe near shore and dump the water, I know an old Indian trick that'll fix us up fast," said Ray, pushing ahead. Leaping over rocks and boulders, he disappeared into the pines that were thick on the island while Lew and Osborne managed the boat. By the time they had the water out, Ray was back, hands sticky with globs of pine pitch. Within seconds he had plugged the bullet holes.

"You think that'll hold?" asked Osborne.

"Long enough to get us to shore," said Ray, shoving the canoe into the water. It floated fine.

"Here's the deal," said Ray. "I've fished this lake so many times—I know the other side of this island extends almost to the shoreline. If we go 'round the island and head in from that side, we can make it across open water in less than a minute—two at the most. That'll put us about five hundred feet from O'Brien's dock and well hidden by trees. Unless he's right *on* the beach, he won't be able to see us—and for all he knows he sunk our boat. I'll bet you anything he's up searching for Molly in the woods behind his place."

They cleared the open water in the minute Ray had predicted. Though they stayed hunkered low in the canoe just in case, there was no gunfire. Osborne and Ray raced to pull the canoe up on shore and had just turned to follow Lew when they heard the sound of tires coming from the direction of O'Brien's cabin. All three stopped.

"Dear God, I hope it's not Todd," said Lew. "He's driving right into trouble."

As they ran along the shoreline toward O'Brien's dock, a car door slammed. Hiding behind a stand of young balsam, they looked up towards the cabin. No sign of Molly—or Jerry O'Brien. No police cruiser either. Only a vintage black Cadillac.

"Damn!" said Lew. "What the hell is Lillie Wright doing out here?"

Before she had finished her sentence, they had the answer. Once, twice, three times a trigger was pulled. They waited at the edge of the woods for a long moment. Then Lew darted across the yard, her Sig Sauer out. Fifty feet from the cabin, she positioned herself behind the thick trunk of a basswood.

"O'Brien—Loon Lake Police. Drop your gun and come out."

The door opened and a stocky figure in black, a

hefty-looking handgun in her right hand, hurried out onto the deck. "Lewellyn! Where's Molly? What did he do to Molly?"

"Lillie! What possessed you? The man has a rifle."

"He *did*," said the old woman. "Came after me with it, too. Wouldn't've shot him otherwise."

"But you have no business—"

"We'll discuss that later. Right now—*where's Molly*?"

Osborne and Ray ran around to the back of the cabin. Lew and Lillie followed. The bathroom window was wide open, the screen on the ground.

"She had to have run straight for the woods," said Ray. "Yep, look at this, Doc." Ray pointed to a spot a few steps from the cabin where the ground, soggy enough from the previous night's rain, held the slight impression of a sneaker.

"Don't worry, Lillie. I'm sure Molly's safe," said Lew. "We heard enough through the walkie-talkies that I'm sure she made it through the window in plenty of time to reach cover. If she didn't, we'd see blood somewhere, and we don't."

"Lew's right," said Osborne. He watched as Lew, who had spotted Molly's backpack on the floor just inside the door to the cabin, reached to pull out the cell phone. "Still on," she said, holding it up like a flag of victory. "Damn good battery."

"What makes you think she's not lost in those woods?" asked Lillie, hands on her hips, cheeks waggling. She reminded Osborne of Rumplestiltskin ready to do the anger dance. "I demand you send out a search team."

"Lillie, we've got the best tracker in the county looking for her. You know what they say about Ray Pradt: The man can see around the corner to tomorrow. Now how 'bout we give him thirty minutes and see what happens. You agree to that?"

Lillie leveled her eyes at Lew, threw her shoulders back as if she was about to argue, then shrugged and said, "Okay."

Molly was still running when Ray caught up to her. It took awhile to calm her down, and it was nearly an hour before they came walking down the drive to O'Brien's cabin. Lillie, sitting on the deck with Osborne, saw them first. She jumped to open the door and holler at Lew who was on the phone with Marlene. "They're here. She looks okay!" She rushed over as Molly climbed the stairs to the deck. "Are you all right, child?"

"Fine. I'm fine. A little shaky. Ray said you shot Jerry. He's dead?"

"Very. I made sure of that," said Lillie.

"Is he inside?" asked Molly. "I—I need to see."

Osborne opened the door to the cabin for Molly to enter. Ray and Lillie followed, as did Osborne. Molly walked to the middle of the room, then stopped to look.

What was left of Jerry O'Brien would have to be sorted out from the cabin wall. Unlike a .22, a .357 leaves little to chance.

As Molly turned to leave, Lillie put an arm across her shoulders. "Better me than you, kid."

"But Lillie, you could have been—" said Molly.

"That's what I said. Better me than you. I've got a full life behind me. You've got a full one ahead."

"It's all over now, isn't it?"

"Yes," said the old woman. "No more nightmares."

thirty-one

You must lose a fly to catch a trout.

—George Herbert

Early the next morning, Osborne had just sat down to a bowl of shredded wheat topped with peach slices when he heard the back door slam. As Ray sauntered in, he threw a thick white envelope, end flap open, on the kitchen table. "Coffee ready?"

"Help yourself. What's that?" asked Osborne, scooping up a spoonful of cereal.

"Those are my photos from 'Fishing for Girls.' Assuming you're recovered from all the excitement, I thought you might enjoy seeing 'em."

"Can I look later? Need to catch up with Lew. You caught me just finishing my breakfast before heading into town." Osborne checked the clock on the wall. "Oh, heck. I got five, ten minutes. Have a seat."

"Oh, yeah, poor Lew," said Ray, filling a mug. "What a bum week this is, huh. Talk about working overtime. Good thing she's running for sheriff—make other people do all the work. Y'know, Doc, the way these storm clouds keep moving through—she's likely to miss a great night for muskie." Ray raised his mug as if to toast the best weather ever for enticing the old shark of the north.

"Say, you got my message about your buddy Darryl? We need to find him—he's the one been helping Hope McDonald all these weeks."

"Sure 'nough." Ray leaned back against the counter. "Doesn't surprise me. Ol' Darryl may be a scary-lookin' son of a gun, but talk about a good heart. Got a joke for your grandchildren, Doc—how come," Ray's eyes twinkled, "there is no mad cauliflower disease?"

Osborne gave him the dim eye. "I don't get it."

"The kids will. Works better with brussels sprouts. Hey—so who are these jabones?" Glancing sideways, Ray pointed his mug at the lab enlargements of the bank robbers, the set Osborne had brought home from Lew's office. He had laid them out on the counter under the bright kitchen lights. Ray scooped up the oversized photos, moved them over to the kitchen table, and plunked himself into a chair.

He sipped his coffee as he studied the photos. "So, Doc, did you hear the one about the jumper cables who stopped by Birchwood Bar the other day?"

"You're in fine form this morning," said Osborne, putting his cereal bowl in the sink and reaching for the coffeepot. He had time for one more cup and one last joke before heading into town to find Lew. If listening meant getting Darryl's address sooner rather than later, he could manage.

"The bartender said, 'I'll serve you—but don't start anything.'"

It was a bad joke, but Osborne chuckled anyway. That was one his grandchildren *would* like. "Here," he said as he turned around, pot in hand, "let me give you a warm-up."

"Thank you, sir," said Ray, holding out his mug. "Every time you do that—the gates of heaven open."

With his left hand, Ray shook his photos out of their envelope. "Just a quick look, Doc. I've got a good shot of you here, you handsome dog.

"And, by the way, think it's too soon to ask Molly out for fish fry?" Ray spread the photos across the table as he spoke.

Osborne, still standing behind him with the coffeepot in one hand, didn't answer. Ray looked up. "What's wrong, Doc?" Osborne set the pot on its burner and turned back to the kitchen table.

"Look at this," he said, sliding one of Ray's photos away from the others. It was a shot of Carla and Barb standing on the pontoon, arms around one another's waists. Carla was grinning at the camera, Barb looked tense. Osborrne set the photo alongside the enlargement of the two masked individuals caught by the surveillance cameras.

"The shape of Carla's head . . . see how unusually small it is . . . and that truncated jaw of hers?" Osborne pointed. "Look how quickly it tapers from cheekbone to chin. You don't see that very often. Now look how similar it is to the bone structure you see on the head in this enlargement."

"I thought you were looking at this," said Ray, pointing at the other figure. "The set of those shoulders. That could be Barb. . . ." The two men leaned close in to examine the photos. Even the difference in height between the two robbers appeared to be identical to that between Carla and Barb. Osborne put down his coffee mug. "Excuse me a minute."

Letting Mike in as he opened the back door, he ran across the yard to the back of his garage, through the fish porch and into the room holding the files from his dental practice. Yanking open a drawer in one of the tall oak file cabinets, he found the years most likely and worked his fingers through the *W*s. Took less than two minutes to find a dental record for Carla at the age of sixteen. He opened the file and . . . yes, he had what he needed. He ran back to the kitchen.

"What'd you find?" asked Ray.

"Took measurements of her jaw when she was a teenager," said Osborne. "I thought I might have. So remarkable to see bone structure like that and not have a kid need orthodonture. Who knows, this might be enough for the Wausau boys to work from—see if they can prove a match. Can I take that photo?"

As Ray handed it over, Osborne tried Lew's direct number at the office. Marlene answered. "She remembered something important she'd forgotten to ask Bunny DeLoye. We tried to reach her by phone, but she was on her morning walk, so Chief Ferris headed out to catch up with her about a half-hour ago," said Marlene. "I'm sure she's still there. Need me to page her?"

"Please," said Osborne. "Have her call me at the house right away."

Within a minute the phone rang. "Doc," said Lew, "what's up?"

He spoke quickly, giving a brief description of the matching photos. As he talked, his eyes caught Ray's. The morning's good humor had given way to an expression of intense concentration.

When he finished, Lew said, "Looks like the day's got Wolniewicz all over it, Doc. I want to find Darryl first. Bunny just told me the only person besides herself who has a key to the McDonald's main gate is the garbage man: Darryl Wolniewicz. I feel like such a dumbyak, Doc—it never occurred to me that the garbage collectors have keys to all these private estates. Ask Ray what's the quickest way out to his place."

"Ray," said Osborne, holding the phone aside, "she needs to find Darryl—now."

"His place is back in off Spider Lake Road. No fire number, no running water. I'll have to show you guys. Hard to find if you don't know where you're going. But no use rushing. He's on the garbage run until eleven. You'd be hard pressed to find him before then. First you have to track down the town chairman, then hope he's got the pick-up schedule somewhere. By the time you do all that, you're better off just waiting for him at his place later this morning. I've done this; I know."

"I heard," said Lew. "Meet you two back at my office as soon as you can get there."

thirty-two

All fish are not caught with flies.

—John Lyly

"The weak link is Barb," said Ray, once Lew had had a chance to examine the photos. "I would start there."

"You think she'll cave?" asked Lew, looking at him from across her desk.

"She gets shook pretty easy," said Ray. "Based on what Doc and I saw when Carla got the message that the IRS was doing an audit—I'd say Carla beats up on her."

"She likes Ray," said Osborne. "Don't know if that helps."

"Here's a thought," said Ray. "Ask Barb why Carla stopped by my place with nine-thousand-nine in hundred dollar bills and is insisting on separate payments for that pontoon. She wants the receipt made out to the realty office, so we can assume Barb knows about it. Ask her why it's so important to stay under the Feds' radar."

"What are we talking about here?" asked Osborne.

"Cash payments of ten thousand dollars or more have to be reported," said Lew.

• • •

When they got to the realty office, Carla's red SUV was nowhere in sight. A forest-green Lincoln Town Car was parked near the front door. Osborne and Ray, in Osborne's station wagon, pulled up alongside Lew's cruiser.

The half-log building was so new, the interior smelled of fresh paint. They entered through a narrow foyer, devoid of furniture, into a carpeted "great room" that featured a wide, rock fireplace at one end and a vaulted ceiling. The room was sparsely furnished. Two large desks, one across from the other, anchored the far end of the room. A scattering of chairs faced each desk.

Barb sat at one of the desks, head bowed over a laptop computer. She hadn't heard them come in. When she did look up, it was obvious she was expecting someone else: someone she feared.

"Well, hey, hello," she said, struggling to her feet as a smile broke through the anxiety on her face. "Ray, Doc, what brings you out here? Carla just left, if you're looking—" Her expression turned serious at the sight of Lew in her uniform.

"Nope, it's all about you, Barb," said Ray, his voice relaxed and genial. "Got a minute?"

She sat back down and pushed the computer aside. "Ray," she said, "for you—all day." As they pulled chairs up to her desk, Osborne could see the strain in her face. She looked as if she hadn't been sleeping. An open bag of corn chips sat next to her laptop.

"Do you know Chief Ferris?"

"I know who you are," said Barb, extending a hand across the table. Lew gave her a friendly smile.

"This is quite a nice place," said Ray, glancing around the room

"Yeah?" Barb's voice was apologetic. "We got furniture on order. Takes forever to get stuff done in this town."

"What's a building like this cost anyway?" asked Ray.

"With the site, which is commercial, and we used a Wausau Home plan, you know—not too bad. Carla has had her dad doing the painting for us so that keeps the costs down. Maybe, oh, little over a million?"

"You girls are doing great."

"I guess we are," Barb said, her voice flat.

Ray smiled at her, his eyes kind. Lew and Osborne sat quietly beside him. A faint humming from a refrigerator somewhere could be heard. Barb shifted in her chair, then fidgeted with her pen. The three visitors watched her. No one said anything.

"Barb . . . we know," said Ray.

Barb looked away from him, fluttered her hands, then pressed the fingers of her right hand to her temple as if she had a headache. After a long, silent moment, she met Ray's gaze. She looked at Osborne and at Lew, then she said, "I'm glad. I can't live this way anymore."

She covered her face with both hands for moment, then heaved a breath. "Okay, where do we start?"

"Where's the money?" asked Ray.

"Carla keeps it in a locker at the casino. She has the key."

"Did you and Carla work together at the credit union?" asked Lew.

"Yes. That's how we became friends. And this whole

bank scheme was an accident, really. Carla decided we'd play a trick on a girlfriend of ours who was a teller at First National in Crandon. We knew she was the only one who worked the lunch hour, so we dressed up, walked in wearing masks, handed her a note that Carla wrote, and expected her to start laughing.

"But she didn't. She handed us everything in her drawer. So . . . we walked out, got in our car, and drove away. No cops, no sirens. No one ever even reported the bank was robbed. We had seventy-five hundred dollars in cash.

"And your friend never knew it was you?"

"No. After that, Carla made the plans. I did what I was told. But—I know . . . I'm going to jail aren't I?"

"Prison," said Lew. "Robbing banks is a federal offense. But the more you tell us, the better it'll be for you. Do you want to call a lawyer?"

"I don't have a lawyer." Barb's face collapsed.

"I can suggest someone who's very good," said Osborne. "Lillie Wright."

Barb looked at Ray for confirmation. He nodded. "I'll call her later," said Barb. "I'll feel better if I get this off my chest before anything else happens."

"You mean the IRS thing?" asked Ray.

"Kinda, yeah." From the way her eyes moved, Osborne knew there was something else worrying her.

As if the confession could cleanse her soul, Barb was more than ready to talk. According to her, it was at Carla's insistence that she had kept a ledger detailing each heist: Every bank robbed, the date and time, the take.

They planned carefully, choosing small banks with

limited staff and hitting late in the morning—in time for the previous day's deposits but before the noon rush. And always happy with modest takes ranging from a few thousand dollars to eighteen or twenty thousand at the most.

"We never did more than one a month," said Barb. "It had to be at least a hundred miles away from our last bank. We made sure to choose a different day of the week, and we had one rule: we had to be able to park our car around a corner so we could drive off without being seen.

"The last bank surprised us," said Barb. "We couldn't believe how much money we got. That's when Carla came up with the idea of opening this realty company—we needed an excuse for why we had so much money."

"Where and how does Ed Kelly figure into this?" asked Osborne. "Didn't I hear that you're the brokers for some land he's selling?"

"Carla met Ed and his girlfriend up at the casino. They were sitting at a blackjack table together, and Carla mentioned she was in real estate. Ed said he had been looking to work with a firm that didn't buy for itself. We had no plans to do that—we just wanted to look like we did *something*. So one thing led to another, y'know. The strange thing is, he brought us more customers, and now we really *are* making a lot of money."

Barb's eyes brimmed with tears. "You know," she said, starting to cry, "I have my real estate license, I enjoy doing this. Why . . . why couldn't all this," she swept her arm around the room, "have happened sooner?"

"Why couldn't you have said no to Carla way back

when?" asked Lew, her voice quiet. "That's the tough question, Barb. You're a nice person in a bad situation."

"I know." Barb wiped at her face. "I guess—I was afraid. That first robbery was supposed to be a fake, and then it was real, and then she told me I was as guilty as her. I was in too deep. You're gonna put in me jail today, right?"

"Yes," said Lew. "I'm afraid I will. And I'm not sure about bail."

Barb leaned forward, her face frightened. "Please don't put me in the same cell with Carla. She went after her dad this morning; I don't need her coming after me next."

"Her father—you mean Darryl?"

"Yeah. Poor guy. She treats him so bad. He was doing a lot of the work here—painting and stuff. Man, is she mean to him. Well, he got her back a hundred times over—he's the one sicced the IRS on us."

"How do you know that?" asked Ray. "He never said any such thing to me."

"A friend of mine heard him bragging at a bar the other night. He was drunk and shooting off his mouth. I told Carla about it this morning—she was furious. Left for his place about an hour ago."

thirty-three

Who hears the fishes when they cry?

—Henry David Thoreau

Ray was right. The road in to Darryl's place was un-marked and hard to spot. If you were headed west, you had less than two seconds to spot the ruts that cut back and east off the road—then a lurching, twisting mile down a grassy lane more logging trail than driveway.

The man lived in a sagging old shack whose logs were so black and its chinking so crumbling that it had to date from the early 1900s. Those were the glory days of the northwoods, when loggers by the thousands built one-room homesteads deep in the woods where they worked. But what might have once been a haven for a hardworking man was today's squatter's paradise: run-down and ramshackle.

"Does he even have running water?" asked Lew, eyeing the shack from a distance, as the police cruiser heaved its way over ruts and rocks.

"No water, wood heat, root cellar," said Ray. "And electricity—he's got electricity. Place is really not all that bad."

"Does he own all this land?" asked Osborne, thinking Darryl could log a few acres and make enough to pay for indoor plumbing.

"Belongs to a guy from Chicago," said Ray. "He lets Darryl live here so long as he keeps hunters and snowmobiles off the property."

The shack appeared deserted until they crested a rise fronting the building. Only then did they spot the red SUV parked alongside a huge, black satellite dish.

"Wouldn't you know," said Lew. "Can't afford a faucet but he's got sixty thousand channels on his goddam TV set." She tipped her head at Osborne. "So ask your daughter. Is this what she has in mind when she tells me I need to get out and shake hands? Track down all these razzbonyas with no fire numbers and big honking satellite dishes?"

"Hey, easy on the insults," said Ray. "So the man's got HBO—lucky dog. Talked him into a cell phone a while back, too. Got tired of trying to reach him by carrier pigeon."

"That's no carrier pigeon driving that SUV," said Osborne. "Most likely one angry woman."

Lew reached for her Sig Sauer, pulling it from its holster. "Carla used a gun during the robberies," she said. "I wouldn't put it past her to be armed or have a weapon in her car."

"Lewelleyn . . ." Osborne placed a hand on her arm. "Be careful."

"Planning on it," she said with a quick pat on his knee. "Same goes for you—both of you."

"I can tell you right now something's wrong," said Ray, leaning in from the backseat and keeping his voice low. "Darryl always comes to that window on the right when he hears a vehicle—and where the hell is his van? I don't see it. We didn't pass it on our way out here. Something's up."

"Where does this road end? Do you know, Ray?" asked Lew. The lane on which they had been driving appeared to continue past the shack.

"At the swamp. There's a heron rookery back in there. Enough water for Darryl to keep minnows and leeches. He loves it back in there."

They approached the only door, which opened into a narrow porch of a room that held an ancient icebox, a wooden worktable piled with rags and tools and half-empty boxes of shotgun shells. Walking to the back, Ray knocked on the interior door. No answer. He turned the knob, pushed open the door, and stuck his head inside.

"Darryl," he said. No answer. He motioned to Lew and Osborne to follow him inside.

The kitchen was separated from the living area by a wall covered with shelves and holding a miscellaneous collection of mixing bowls, pots and pans, and food supplies. A wood-burning stove and a wide table covered with a green oilcloth and hosting four rickety wooden chairs crowded the remaining space. It smelled of wood smoke and bacon.

"Hey, Darryl," said Ray again, "you got company." He walked to where the kitchen opened into the next room, which was long and dark.

The windows were so few and tiny and let in so little light that it was difficult to see. The heavy cloud cover outdoors didn't help. Ray reached for a light switch. A single bulb went on over two bunk beds to their immediate right. Osborne could make out a rock fireplace and some furniture in the shadows to their left. A rumpled double bed at the far end made it obvious where Darryl spent most of his time. A large-screen TV rested on a dresser at the foot of the bed.

Lew caught her breath and pointed. Osborne peered past her into the shadows. An old rocking chair and a well-worn wing chair were positioned on a dark rag rug to face the fireplace. A console from the fifties, the kind that held a twelve-inch TV and a turntable, buttressed the seating area, almost hiding two feet, toes facing upward and one foot lacking its sandal.

As they walked across the room, an end table next to the rocking chair came into view. On it was a sawed-off shotgun. "Ever see that before?" asked Lew.

"Oh, yeah," said Ray. "Darryl's had it since he was a kid. Sixteen gauge."

As they neared the console, Lew put her arms out as if to stop Ray and Osborne from going any farther. It was good she did. The rug was changing color.

Edging their way around for a better view, Osborne's first thought was there'd be no measuring Carla's jaw now—never good what a shotgun does to the human head. Lew made an automatic move to check for a pulse. As she did so, she pointed to the revolver gripped tightly in Carla's right hand.

Ray turned on the floor lamp next to the rocking chair. The light illuminated more blood—a pattern leading across the wood floor and toward the door that led out of the back of the building. Bolting through the door, Ray ran down the rutted lane into the woods behind the shack, shouting, "Darryl! I'm here. Hold on, it's Ray!"

Osborne followed him, while Lew hurried to radio for assistance.

They found the van a quarter mile down the road at the edge of the swamp. Ray yanked open the driver's-side door. He was leaning in as Osborne caught up.

"He's alive, Doc. Bleeding bad, but he's alive."

To kill a human being—yourself or someone else—with one shot from a .22 pistol requires excellent aim. Darryl must have jerked as he pulled the trigger because he missed his heart and shattered a shoulder blade. Nevertheless, he was in pain and bleeding.

"Omigod, Ray," he said with a gurgle, "I won't make it, 'ol buddy. I shot the main artery to my heart."

"No, you didn't, Darryl," said Ray, ripping off his shirt and pressing it hard against the wound in Darryl's chest.

"I shot her—I wanna die. You gotta let me die."

"Help me hold him, Doc," said Ray, wrestling Darryl out of the van seat and onto the ground. "Now you just lay quiet, the ambulance is on its way."

"I shot her—"

"We know you shot her, big guy. No doubt about it. But it sure as hell looks like self-defense. So just stop talking and everything will be okay."

"No," Darryl twisted his big head with an agony that didn't come from his gunshot wound. His red eyes filled with anguish. "I didn't understand, I didn't know. I shot Hope. I killed Missus McDonald." He passed out.

Ray dropped his head, then looked up, heartbreak written across his face. Osborne knew that look. It's the look you have when the people you love are in trouble and there's nothing you can do to help.

"Doc, he's lost it. He's in shock. We didn't hear anything." Ray pressed his shirt hard on Darryl's chest, just above his heart. His face took on a grim resolve as he said, "Darryl did not shoot Hope McDonald. I'll bet my life on that."

"I'd like to believe you," said Osborne, staring down at a brown-red face gone white.

thirty-four

Always let your hook be hanging; where you least expect it; there will swim a fish.

—Ovid

"**He's** still pretty shaken, but the doc said talking's not going to do any damage," said Ray. Lew and Osborne had arrived at the hospital an hour after the ambulance ride. They found Ray sitting in a hospital room, his chair pulled up next to Darryl's bed.

"That bullet wound looked worse than it was," said Ray, standing up as they walked in. "The emergency room doc gave him a local and patched him up in less 'n twenty minutes. But they want him overnight for observation—blood pressure's high."

"That's better than I was expecting to hear," said Lew, glancing over to where Darryl lay propped up on pillows. He looked markedly less fierce in a lilac hospital gown with a white blanket tucking him in up to his chest. He gave a weak smile. Osborne made a mental note to arrange for some new front teeth—for free.

"You feel good enough to talk to us, Mr. Wolniewicz?" asked Lew, pulling a chair up beside Ray's and close to Darryl. Osborne found a chair in the hall. He set himself down on the other side of Ray.

"Darryl," said Darryl, wheezing. His weather-beaten face and lumbering body appeared dwarfed under the harsh light of the hospital room. "Call me Darryl. Guess you'll put me away, for sure, huh."

"I don't know. Until you tell me what happened, I can't tell you what will happen." Lew was brisk but friendly. "Before I spend money sending those guns of yours down to Wausau for ballistics testing, I thought we could chat, get a few things straight."

Darryl laid his head back on the pillow, defeat in his face. "I shot Missus McDonald, if that's what you want to know. If only Carla hadn't—" He raised his fists to his face, gnarled knuckles pressed hard against his eye sockets.

Osborne looked away, expecting a sob. But, after a pause, what he heard was a whisper: "Okay, but I—I'd like you all to know that I—I—I didn't mean to do it."

Halting, stuttering at times, his fingers twisting the hospital bedding, he told his story.

"Kinda started last March when I cut some trees for Missus McDonald, y'know. She liked my work, and I didn't charge too much, and so's she asked me if I'd come back and cut some more. So I did, y'know. I saw she had more things needed fixin'. So's I stained that deck of hers, too. She was not feelin' too good some days, so's I'd help her out with things in the house at times, y'know."

"Is that when she gave you a key to the front gate?" asked Lew.

"No, no, I got keys to all the private gates in the township—for garbage pick-up."

"*Ahhh*," said Lew. "You could come and go at the McDonalds' whenever you needed. Is that right?"

"Yep. Didn't bother Missus McDonald, if that's what you mean. She wanted me there."

He took a deep breath. "Couple a months ago, I guess it was early April, she asked me into the house, and we had a talk. She told me she was very sick, that she was likely to check out pretty soon, but she wanted to do one thing. She wanted to build herself a gazebo. She wanted to build this gazebo to sleep out there this summer like she used to sleep in the old boathouse when she was a kid—the one they had to tear down 'cause of the shoreline regs. . . . I guess, well, my thinking was she wanted to die there.

"She asked me how much it would cost for me to build it fast." Darryl sat up straighter. "Y'see, maybe Ray told you, I had a lotta work this spring. I had my garbage route, then I was doing painting for Carla. So, first thing, I told Carla she'd have to wait a little while I did the project for Missus Hope. That made her mad, 'course—"

"Of course," said Lew.

"But what the hell—"

"I hear you, Darryl, 'what the hell.' So you were doing work for Carla in that new building of hers this past spring?"

"Yeah, but she was only paying me five bucks an hour, and Missus Hope said if I built that gazebo fast, she'd pay me a lot more'n five bucks an hour. And she's a hell of a lot nicer to me than that goddam daughter of mine.

"So I'm started on the gazebo, see, and meanwhile Carla's madder 'n hell and starts calling me and swearing on the phone. Seems she met some guy, and all of a sudden she needs the work done that day, y'know. But I stuck with Missus Hope. I got all the lumber and we decided on a plan. . . ." The hands twisted the blanket.

"She was so excited." Darryl smiled as he spoke. "She was like a little kid, y'know. She'd come down and talk to me while I worked. She liked to hear how I catched bluegills in this one spot in that channel that feeds into her lake. Fact, one day I drove her over there in that old van o'mine—showed her right where I put my boat in."

"Now, this is on her property, isn't it?" said Lew.

"Yeah, but didn't seem to bother her at all."

"Were other people around during this time—or were you always alone with Mrs. McDonald?" asked Lew.

"Most of the time alone. She didn't want people around is what she told me. I know I heard her cussin' out that daughter of hers."

"Any idea why?" asked Lew.

"Hell, no. What do I know about daughters—look at the mess I made. Sure as hell not gonna bring *that* up.

"All I know is Missus Hope was getting kinda dreamy. She wasn't paying attention all the time. Just kept eating potato chips. One day last week she opened all the windows in her house and let the wind blow papers every which way. I was worried she'd lose something important, so I made sure to help her straighten up. Her office 'specially. She had bags of potato chips everywhere and those things are greasy. She shouldn't have that on her paperwork."

"Oh, that answers a question," said Lew. "I wondered who cleaned up her office."

"That was me. . . ." Darryl waited to see if Lew had another question, but she waved him on. "Yeah, so one day last month I was working on the gazebo when she walked down from the big house and told me she had a present for me. She gave me this piece of paper with her lawyer's name and phone number on it. Told me to call because she was giving me the land right along the channel—right where I been catching bluegills."

"Darryl, you didn't tell *me* about this," said Ray.

"I didn't tell anybody 'cept Carla. Missus Hope made me promise not to tell anyone until later—after she died. Told me she didn't want any brouhaha, y'know."

"So you saw the lawyer, and what did he say?" asked Lew.

"She. Her lawyer's this old lady. She did the paperwork and gave me the deed, and I gave that to Carla and asked her to have it recorded."

"Are you kidding?" Ray broke in. "Why on earth would you give that to Carla—the way she treats you?"

"Well . . . I thought . . . the lawyer told me I had to get it recorded and a real estate agent could help me do that. You know Carla's got her real estate license."

Listening, Osborne suspected Darryl might have had the urge to show off. Demonstrate to his unappreciative offspring that he, too, was a person of property. *Expensive* property.

"Yes, we know about Carla and her real estate license," said Lew.

"Damn it, Darryl, if you'd only told me," said Ray.

"You probably could've walked it into the title company and done it yourself."

"I didn't know that," said Darryl. "And it was a big mistake. Carla refused to do it until I finished the painting. Then, when I did finish, she said I did a lousy job and refused to pay me. I didn't take that real well. She made Barb cry that day, too. That's when I decided I would fix her wagon good."

"Darryl," said Ray, "stop for a second. Take a minute to tell Chief Ferris how Carla has treated you all these years."

Darryl dropped his head to one side as if he had been struck. "She tells me I'm disgusting. Whenever she talks to me—she has this sneer on her face. She just always treats me with . . . what's that word you use, Ray?"

"Contempt."

"Yeah, y'know, contempt."

Lew shook her head, "So you decided to fix her wagon."

"Yeah, I been seein' her flash money around for over a year now. Barb told me she paid their builder in cash. He's the one first mentioned turning her into the IRS. She cut her bill with him in half, y'know. Refused to pay him. He was cursing, told me the IRS pays bounties to hear about people with too much cash. I happen to know she bought both them cars with cash, too."

"And the pontoon," said Ray.

"Yeah, see. So I figured she wasn't paying her taxes, and I was just mad as hell. One night after I had too many brewskies, I called the IRS's eight-hundred number and told 'em I thought they should check into Carla."

"Was this an anonymous tip?" asked Lew.

"They said they needed my name," said Darryl. "But they didn't tell nobody. My own fault—I was drunk the other night and got to bragging 'bout what I did. Ever'body in the goddam bar heard me, doncha know. Guess some one o'those folks got hold of Barb and told her what I been sayin'. So that's how come Carla came out to my place today. She found out I was the one squealed on her. Barb called me and said she was on her way and real mad. So I pulled out my shotgun. I just meant to scare her—I knew what she would do.

"And she did it, too. She busted right into my place and started hitting on me—"

"Hitting you?" asked Lew. "So that's when you shot her?"

"No, I shot her after she told me what she did. She never registered my title—she sold my land is what she did. She stole it and sold it to somebody else."

"But you didn't know that until this morning?"

"I thought Missus McDonald had changed her mind. See, I went out there early last week to walk the property line and make my plans and stuff. And this woman shows up and kicks me off. Says it's her place—that she just bought it."

"Did she say who she was?"

"Not at first, she was real snotty, but I scared her when I wouldn't back off. I told her it was my property, and I'd see her in court if she kept it up. That's when she gave me her name and said I could check the records at the county clerk's office. Woman's name is Julia somebody."

"Not Julia Wendt?" asked Osborne.

"Yeah—that's the one!" said Darryl. "Julia Wendt.

How do you know her, Doc? She's the one Carla sold my land to—the bitch. Well, when she told me that— it was over. It was all over."

Darryl leveled red eyes at Lew, then Ray. "I don't care anymore. Two weeks ago I was the happiest man in the world. Now . . . nothin'. I got nothin' and I killed a beautiful lady who was so good to me. . . ."

Darryl broke down, sobbing. Deep, anguished sobs. Lew waited. Ray got up to walk over and rub his shoulders, handing him a Kleenex box from the hospital tray.

"I need to hear from you what happened at the McDonalds'," said Lew.

"I know, I know, I'm sorry," said Darryl, wheezing and blowing his nose. When he could speak, he said, "It was Saturday when that Julia woman kicked me off my property. I was upset—knew I couldn't do anything about it till Monday anyway. So I was at my place Sunday afternoon. . . ."

"Drinking," said Ray. "You were pretty soused, Darryl. Do you remember me calling you?"

"You called me, then Missus McDonald called and told me some squirrels had gotten into the gazebo, and she wanted me to come over and git 'em out of there. So I got my twenty-two 'cause I always shoot the suckers with a pistol, and I went over.

"When I got there, I didn't see any squirrels so I went up to the house, and she was there. About ready to eat something, I guess. I'd had enough pops that afternoon, I decided to ask her why she changed her mind on that property.

"Maybe it was the way I said it, I dunno, but she just—she started screaming at me. Kept calling me 'Ed.' Then all of a sudden she came at me like my wife used to. Like Carla does. All of a sudden, it wasn't her face in front of me. It was my wife all over again. She came at me, I shoved her back in her chair. And I emptied the goddam gun. . . but I swear I thought I was shooting my wife."

The room was quiet. "Then you drove home?"

"I guess I did. I don't remember. The minute she started raging at me like that, I blanked out until the next morning."

"Then what did you do?"

"It was Monday—I went to work. I just kept hoping it was all a bad dream. All of it, y'know. That I'd wake up and have this beautiful land by the lake . . . that this nice lady would keep wantin' me to build stuff . . . that I could catch my bluegills. . . ."

thirty-five

. . . And, finally, I fish not because I regard fishing as being terribly important, but because I suspect that so many of the other concerns of men are equally unimportant, and not nearly so much fun.

—John Voelker (Robert Traver)

The morning sun helped, but it was a swath of white running along its base that made the old courthouse appear freshly painted. It wasn't until Osborne had parked across the street and was walking toward the entrance to the police department that he could make out the details of the giant white tent.

Television camera crews were setting up, running cable, chatting, drinking from large paper cups of coffee. Two satellite television trucks had crammed themselves into the police department's small parking lot. Osborne was surprised not to see Ray with the stuffed trout on his head schmoozing, doing his best to con a cameraman into using him for local color.

Osborne leaned back against a tree, eager to watch Lew directing the media. She had set eight-thirty *sharp* for the general press conference. At the moment, she was instructing reporters from the *Loon Lake Daily News* and Rhinelander's only television station, Channel 12, to take chairs in the front row.

"How does it look, Dad?" Osborne jumped at the sound of Erin's voice.

"What are you doing here, kiddo?"

"Chief Ferris called early this morning and asked me if I'd help set up this press conference. We've been running around like crazy to get these chairs, the podium—even got a press release ready. Not bad for ninety minutes' notice, doncha think? Oh, here she comes . . . shush." Erin held a finger to her lips as Lew stepped up to the mike.

She opened with a brief statement of fact: Darryl Wolniewicz, a Loon Lake resident, had confessed to an alleged "accidental" shooting of his employer, the internationally known advice columnist Hope Mc-Donald.

"Loon Lake is as saddened as her readers worldwide must be at this time," said Lew, "but as Chief of the Loon Lake Police, I must emphasize that her death appears to be the result of a tragic accident. An inquest will be held and details will be made available at that time. Thank you."

For another few minutes, Lew took questions from the two local reporters. She then referred the remaining twenty-plus members of the press to the information in the press release. Half a dozen hands shot up but Lew shook her head, refusing to answer any more questions. "If you need additional background, you can work with the local reporters," she said, "or you can reach Hope McDonald's husband, Ed Kelly, at the Claridge Inn in Rhinelander. He ought to be awake by now."

She gave a room number and a phone number—upon which at least a dozen reporters punched numbers into their cell phones as they raced for their vehicles. Osborne could swear he saw a twinkle in Lew's eye.

"Now if you'll excuse me," she said, "I have other work to do. Thank you." She exited to a chorus of shouted questions.

"Darn it, Dad," said Erin with a thrust of her lower lip. "I told her to take questions from the national media—she could have been on CNN tonight! You know, I have to wonder if she really wants to be somebody."

He was inclined to agree with Erin. What *was* Lew thinking? How many people turned down the chance to be on national television? How many people *running for office* turn down television? He was beginning to think she meant it when she said she was dropping out of the race.

"Lew, I was flabbergasted not to see Ray out there working the media," said Osborne half an hour later. It had not been difficult to talk Lew into a quick cup of coffee given that her day had started at dawn. "He must be losing his touch—he's usually first in line to offer local color for what he likes to call B-roll."

Lew laughed. "I didn't think about that. I sent Ray and Roger up to the casino early this morning. They're due back any minute with what I hope is a couple million in cash of the tribe's money. I need to be here when that walks in the door."

"So Barb was telling the truth," said Osborne.

"She's been very cooperative. Said we'd find a key

in Carla's purse, and we did—but not until late last night. I drafted Ray first thing this morning—"

"Good thing he didn't know you'd have national TV—not just the locals."

"Ouch, I didn't think about that," said Lew. "He'll never forgive me."

"Well, Lew," said Osborne, raising his coffee mug in a mock toast, "you should be very pleased. Can't get much better than being able to tell Ed Kelly and his daughter what happened to Hope—not to mention getting a few dollars back for the tribe. Two cases resolved in one day—that has to be a record."

"Luck. Sheer luck."

"C'mon now. You know that old saying: 'fortune favors the prepared mind.' You know what Erin said about you when you decided to run for sheriff? She said, 'Dad, Lew can win. She's the kind of person that makes things happen.'"

Lew's expression changed. Relaxed and happy a moment ago, she now seemed tense. She took a final swig of her coffee and reached for a stack of papers on her desk. Osborne could see it was time for him to be on his way.

What on earth did I say wrong? Osborne asked himself as he left the office. He was still shaking his head as he pulled into his driveway.

thirty-six

Heaven seems a little closer in a house beside the water.

—Anonymous

Though Osborne had scored miserably on his pop quiz as to *why* the women in "Fishing for Girls" wanted to fish, Ray made good on the thimbleberry pies. Delicious. And everyone around the table agreed: his piecrust was out of this world—flaky, buttery, toasted to a golden brown perfection. As Ray basked in the compliments, Osborne stretched his legs, leaned back in his chair, and glanced over at Lew, contentment in his heart.

He had decided at the last minute to host a potluck picnic on his deck. Knowing Lew would have spent the day mired in paperwork, he called her first. Then Lillie, who accepted with enthusiasm, saying she knew that Molly, too, would appreciate a break from dealing with the legalities surrounding O'Brien's death. Molly might be safe from Jerry, but their marriage made her his closest relative, even in death. Ray, he knew without asking, could be counted on.

Perhaps because the evening air was a balmy seventy degrees, his company had arrived early. Lew brought cheese and crackers—a three-year sharp Wisconsin cheddar—then volunteered to help him grill venison burgers. Molly and Lillie picked up two quarts of the Loon Lake Market's "homemade recipe" potato salad. And Ray, the perfect pies.

"That Ed Kelly," said Lillie, holding court as Molly and Ray cleared the table. "I got hold of the state's attorney general today. They'll put a lid on that no-good son of a gun." Again her fierce righteousness triggered an image of the great horned owl perched high in the pines overhead: both relished the taste of blood.

"What was he planning to do with that land he stole from Darryl?" asked Ray. "I've been so busy with the fishing clinic that starts tomorrow, I didn't hear the latest. By the way, Doc, hope I can count on you for some assistance with this new group of gals."

Osborne gave his neighbor the dim eye. "Surely, you jest. I need a year to recover from the last one."

"Ah, you old razzbonya—you'll come 'round," said Ray with a dismissive wave of his hand. He gave Molly a smile and a wink. She glowed.

"I'm serious. I wouldn't count on it," said Osborne. He was already planning to give Erin a hand with Lew's brochures. Time was running out to reach voters beyond the Loon Lake town limits.

"Ray—you want to hear this or not?" asked Lillie. "Listen to me now because you might know some other folks who've been approached by these people. I'm talking about the Conservation Foundation."

"Madam, you have my full attention," said Ray. "But the Conservation Foundation? Are you sure? Last heard they're into protecting the environment—setting up nature trails, that kind of stuff."

"Ah, ha!" said Lillie, turning a triumphant eye to Lew. "Didn't I just tell you? Those stinkers. They even got Ray conned."

"Oh, no!" said Ray, grimacing in mock confusion. Molly pulled her chair closer to his. Osborne thought he saw their hands graze one another between the chairs. "Might I need to be rescued?"

"You can kid all you want," said Lillie, "but this is serious. What they've been doing is approaching elderly people who own premium property up here, and saying that if the original owners will sell what they call an 'easement' to the foundation, the foundation will take it over and see to protecting the wildlife with nature preserves and so forth. However, once a landowner agrees to the easement, that property now belongs to the foundation to do with as they please.

"What they neglect to mention is they have the right to deny public access and to resell the property to private individuals. Those new owners then have the right to build whatever they want and make any changes they wish in order to have—and this is in the contract language—*enjoyment of views*.

"So what you're saying is the word *easement* really means an out-and-out land sale. Is that right?" asked Ray.

"Right. But it gets more interesting when you look at the new owners. And, by the way, I got this information from an investigative reporter down in Madison who's been looking into the foundation's activities in the southern part of the state.

"The new owners aren't people like you and me they're wealthy people on the foundation's board. They scout the land they want, then have the foundation ap proach the owners, make the deal, and resell it for much less money to the interested board member. The board member pays a much lower price, a fraction of what the foundation paid, then makes a donation to the foundation to cover the gap and *takes a tax deduction for the donation*!

"Up until yesterday, Ed Kelly thought Darryl's land had been sold to the foundation for $600,000 and was in the process of being resold to a certain party in Madison for $100,000. That party was planning to make a donation of half a million—and take the half-million-dollar tax break. Neat, huh. So happens the 'certain party' was Ed himself using a straw buyer."

"Let me guess," said Osborne. "The straw buyer was Julia Wendt?"

"Yes, indeed," said Lillie. "The girlfriend. He also had a handy-dandy list of friends, all on the foundation's board, who were working through Carla and Barb to get their mitts on some other choice properties in the town of Newbold and a couple places up in Boulder Junction. But Ed's goal was to, piece by piece, sell parcels of land from the McDonald Trust—and buy them back through his straw.

"But it's all on hold now. And if I have anything to say about it, you won't see the Conservation Foundation operating in this state ever!"

"Remind me never to be the object of your ire," said Ray. Lillie laughed her throaty laugh.

"Mr. Pradt, you stick to your pies and fishing, and we'll get along just fine. To be perfectly honest, I'm sitting here feeling lucky tonight. Ed knew the one loophole in Hope's will. The McDonald Trust has long supported conservation, and the so-called easement was worded in such a way that he might have gotten away with it for a good while. No more. Not only that, Hope rewrote her will so he gets next to nothing from her. Everything goes to Kitsy."

"Isn't it amazing how human nature has a way of tripping people up?" asked Lew. "Take Carla. There she is not getting around to registering the deed for Darryl, when Ed shows up and makes her an offer she can't refuse. If she hadn't been so greedy, neither of them might have been caught.

"You know," said Lew, looking around the table, "you have to ask yourself what possesses a woman, who has three million dollars in unmarked bills hidden away in a duffle bag, to spend a lousy three thousand bucks that look funny. Why take the risk? Why not just throw those bills away?"

"Why refuse to pay your old man the two hundred and thirty-two dollars you owe him for working nights to paint your office?" asked Ray. "Jeez Louise."

"Greed and sheer meanness," said Lillie. "Takes 'em down every time."

"Poor Darryl," said Ray.

"He'll do okay," said Lillie. "I'm taking him on pro bono like I always do. Got an excellent precedent in a case down in Kansas City with a similar situation. Man shot his stepbrother in the midst of a flashback memory from childhood—got off on temporary insanity. Worth a try, I think."

"What about Barb?" asked Ray. "She needs a good lawyer."

"I can't help her," said Lillie, "though I did give her the names of some lawyers to call."

"She doesn't have any money," said Lew. "Maybe,

since we found close to two million dollars in the duffle, which has been returned to the tribe's insurance company, she'll benefit from having helped with that. Not financially, just a shorter sentence."

"It's a high-profile case," said Lillie. "Some young lawyer will take it."

"How is Kitsy doing?" asked Ray. "I need to give her a call. She wanted me to take her out for a day and show her how to use all that fishing equipment she's planning to buy—"

"Oh, I wouldn't count on that, Ray. That was before everything happened," said Lillie. "She's up to her ears taking over her mother's column—and the business. Kitsy stopped by my office this morning to discuss some estate matters. She said that the response from readers has been overwhelming. The office in Madison is overflowing with flowers, and they've received thousands of letters and e-mails. Early signs are that the readers and the newspapers all want her to keep her mother's column going."

"Does she know her father was seeing Julia?" asked Osborne.

"Oh, yes. While she's not moving too fast, I believe Ed will find himself spending *all* his days on the golf course. If he can afford it. You can't divorce a father," Lillie leaned forward, her cheeks waggling, "but you sure as hell can fire him."

"Doggone," said Ray. "I mean, I'm happy for Kitsy but, jeez, I thought I was gonna make some real money for a change. Now I even got that pontoon back. Gotta sell that all over again."

"Wait just a minute," said Molly. "I need a new rod, some lures—and you can sign me up for an advanced clinic. Play your cards right—maybe *I'll* buy the pontoon."

Everyone around the table burst into laughter. Osborne shook his head. Ray was right: Molly happy was as pretty as a forget-me-not.

"You know," Molly said, "my divorce papers were still on Lillie's desk, so the bulk of Jerry's estate is mine. And it's a lot of money. I want to use some to establish scholarships for students on the reservation. In memory of that kid who was wrongly accused. Some small way of giving back."

"Molly," said Ray, patting her hand, "do that first. Then we'll see about the pontoon."

"Well, folks," said Lillie, setting both palms on the table. "Time to go home. It's been one hell of a week." She got slowly to her feet. "Chief Ferris, I have something for you." She reached back for her purse, opened it, and pulled out a check. "A donation to your campaign."

"Hear, hear," said Osborne, standing up and raising his can of Coke. "I've been waiting to make an announcement myself. I have some news about the campaign that Lew doesn't even know yet. Been waiting for the right moment.

"Erin called this afternoon to say that the tribe is so pleased with the efforts of the current chief of the Loon Lake Police Department that they are making a contribution earmarked to buy a week of television ads. You know what that means, Lew—less time you have to spend shaking hands!"

Lew looked down at her hands in her lap, then up to meet Osborne's eyes. "Doc, everyone, I've decided not to run. I'll announce Monday that I'm dropping out of the race. No," she added, raising a hand as Osborne started to protest, "I have two very good reasons."

"And the first is . . . ?" asked Lillie with a challenging waggle.

"The first is how I feel about how the McDonald case has turned out. Ed Kelly is the person most responsible for Hope's death. He's the one who should be in jail—not Darryl Wolniewicz. He knew how ill his wife was. She should never have been left alone.

"And Julia Wendt lying about Kitsy? Thank goodness the housekeeper was able to document cars coming and going because I was *this* close," Lew crooked her thumb and index fingers, "to arresting Kitsy. Given her emotional state, that could have pushed her right over the edge . . . you know?"

"What are you trying to say, Lew?" asked Osborne. "That you did a bad job? Some things are beyond your control."

"Beyond your responsibilities within the law," said Lillie. "You think *you* feel bad about Hope McDonald. I ask myself every morning why *I* didn't demand she have full-time care out there."

"Chief Ferris," said Ray, "may I remind you of the old Loon Lake proverb. . . ."

Lew cut her eyes towards Ray. "This better be good, guy."

"Perfect is the enemy of good enough."

"So, Lew," Osborne asked, "what's the second reason?"

"If I'm elected sheriff, I become an administrator. An inside-the-office-all-day-every-day desk jockey. And, yes, Lillie is right—this was a hell of a week. But, you know, I love my job. I don't want to give this up. I don't want an office over in Rhinelander and seven reports—or whatever the hell it is.

"I want to work here, I want to be able to play hooky when I need to. Go fishing when I want. . . ."

No one chose to argue that point.

"I have a question for you, Lillie," said Lew as she and Osborne walked the lawyer to her car. Molly and Ray had left for Ray's and a moonlight ride on the pontoon. "You've seen so much crime in your career. What drives a person like Jerry O'Brien? I don't mean the fact that he was gay or the cross-dressing. It's the other, the cold-blooded killing."

"How the hell would I know?" asked Lillie, sliding onto the car seat. "As often as I've been able to predict *what* was going to happen, based on years of observing human behavior, I can't tell you *why*. Wish I could. The only person I really know is myself. And I'm not sure I always know why I do some things."

"You put yourself in grave danger yesterday," said Lew.

"For that, I have no regrets. He had it coming. And I left nothing to chance."

"What do you think she meant by that?" asked Lew as Lillie drove off.

"Exactly what she said," said Osborne.

"So, Lewellyn," said Osborne as they finished up in the kitchen, "you have a birthday coming up. . . ."

"Doc, my age is an unlisted number—so is my birthday." She put her hands on her hips and tried hard to give him an angry look. "Who told you?"

He crossed his arms and leaned back against the

counter with a satisfied grin on his face. "I have it in my office files from years ago."

"All right, all right. So it's the fourth of July. What are you up to?"

"Got a problem with surprises?"

"Nooo."

"Okay, then. It's a date." He would call Ralph in the morning with his plan. If she tried to buy that St. Croix Legend Elite fly rod herself, Ralph was to say he was sold out.

"This was a fun evening, Doc."

He couldn't agree more: the night was fun. The *entire* night was fun.

The Loon Lake Fishing mystery series

by

VICTORIA HOUSTON

You'll be hooked by the first page.

Dead Frenzy	0-425-18887-6
Dead Water	0-425-18003-4
Dead Creek	0-425-17355-0
Dead Angler	0-425-17703-3
Dead Hot Mama	0-425-19332-2

"A GREAT GETAWAY."
—LAURA LIPPMAN

Catch 'em wherever books are sold or at
www.penguin.com

LYN HAMILTON

ARCHAEOLOGICAL MYSTERIES

"Hamilton's archaeological mysteries [are] sure to have
armchair travelers on the edge of their
settees. At once erudite and entertaining...
jaunty whodunits."
—*New York Times Book Review*

Available wherever books are sold or at
www.penguin.com